Praise for the Lily Gayle Lambert Mystery series

"...a charming southern cozy chocked full of engaging characters, laugh out loud humor, and inviting small town charm." **Kathi Daley, Author of the Zoe Donovan Cozy Mysteries**

"...fast-paced and funny. A true Southern mystery with a flavor as authentic as sweet tea." **Jenna Bennett, Author of the Savannah Martin mysteries.**

"...Ms. Boles is a master baker of cozy mysteries. The multiple story elements are mixed together just right and make Cherry Cake and a Cadaver a worthy addition to the series and a tasty read in its own right." **Back Porchervations**

"The characters are always well done and the setting described where the reader thinks they are in the story. You will find yourself turning the pages quickly to see what kind of trouble Lily gets herself into. The secondary characters are just as good and keep the laughter flowing. You will be kept guessing until the end." **Babs Book Bistro**

Also By Susan Boles

Lily Gayle Lambert mystery series

Death of a Wolfman

Cherry Cake and a Cadaver

Death at the Midnight Dragonfly

Death said the Gypsy Queen

Death on the Beach (March 2019)

Historical

Sins of the Mother

Romantic Suspense

Fated Love

Brotherhood Protectors World

Persuading Piper

Handling Harley Ann (October 2018)

Guarding Holly Grace (November 2018)

Death said the Gypsy Queen

A Lily Gayle Lambert Mystery

Susan Boles

Argent Ocean Publishing

An Argent Ocean Publishing book
Copyright 2018

Copyright Susan Boles 2018

ISBN **978-0-9979093-9-5**

CHAPTER ONE

"That oughta be illegal."

I glanced at my best friend, Dixie Newsom; then back at the poppy red 1965 Mustang convertible revealed in the bright sunlight cascading into the open storage unit.

"You're right." I said. "And we're here to set her free. Eight years is too long to be locked up like this." I dangled a key chain between us, glancing at the man who stood quietly a few feet away.

"Thank you for taking care of her all these years, Brad. She looks just like new."

Death said the Gypsy Queen

Brad cleared his throat. "I took her out for a run every couple of months." He glanced at the car. "You can't leave a car sitting for a long time and think it'll be fine to drive when you come back. Especially one like this."

Wasn't *that* a metaphor for just about everything in life?

"I truly appreciate everything, Brad. I was such a mess when I put this car into storage. I can't begin to tell you how much it meant to me back then that you stepped up and offered to take care of the car and everything related to it."

I took a deep breath, trying to bolster my courage.

"But it's high time I got over my fear of driving. John being killed in that car wreck really shook me up back then. I overreacted and now it's time to wrestle that fear down where it belongs."

Dixie put a hand on my arm. "We're all here for you. And I've known you since we were in diapers. This is the only thing I've ever seen throw you. High time to let that fear stop choking you."

I reached up and wiped a bead of sweat out from under my bangs. I didn't know if it'd been brought on by the prospect of driving again after eight years or the not unusual heat of a September afternoon in Oxford, Mississippi.

A roar of sound rose in the distance and we all turned our heads to look at each other and smiled.

"Ole Miss must've scored." Brad remarked, looking with longing in the direction of the sound.

Football season had begun in the SEC; and Ole Miss Fans, students and

alumni filled the town to splitting –
and the stadium situated half a mile
away from us.

"We're holding you up from the
game." Dixie said. "Why don't you go on
before you miss any more of it? We'll
be fine."

Brad glanced in the direction of
the stadium with longing in his eyes,
then back at the two of them. "Weeeell.
If y'all are really sure…"

"Of course we are, Brad." I told
him and gave him a quick hug. "I'm sorry
we're keeping you from the opening."

"I'm surprised y'all aren't at
the game yourselves."

I winced. I hadn't attended a game
in years. Eight years to be exact, and
just thinking about The Grove made me
feel a little nauseated. Those things
had belonged to John and me; and I
hadn't quite gotten to the point where
I felt like I could go to them without

him. Maybe someday that would change. Today was not that day.

Plenty of people tell me I'm being ridiculous, but I don't care. I'm entitled to feel the way I feel.

Today is a big step forward. My recently burgeoning feelings for Vlad Templeton are another step forward. Those are enough for now.

I watched Brad hotfoot it over to his own car, swerve into a U-turn and speed off in the direction of Vaught-Hemingway Stadium.

"Bless his heart." Dixie said. "He's a good man to meet us over here on game day."

I watched Brad's car disappear into the distance. "Yes. He's been a good friend."

"How did he come to be taking care of your car?"

I turned to look at the car in question. Sunlight bounced into my eyes off the gleaming red paint and chrome trim. "He was a big friend of John's and mine back in the day. And when I realized after John died that I'd developed such a fear of driving, he stepped in and promised to take care of it until I got my feet back under me." Tears misted my eyes and I brushed them away quick, hoping Dixie didn't notice. "I'm sure he never dreamed it'd be this long, though."

Dixie clapped her hands together, startling me.

"It's hot out here. Let's get this show on the road."

I walked over to the the car that I'd loved so much once upon a time, opened the door and slid into the leather driver's seat. It fit my butt as though made for me. As I raised my right hand to adjust the rearview mirror, I noticed a slight tremble.

Lord. Please help me today. It's time.

Closing my eyes, I took a few deep breaths. In through the nose. Out through the mouth. Ignoring my racing heart, I did a few more. Feeling a bit more settled I opened my eyes. Still good. Using my left hand, I adjusted the side mirror. No tremor. Good.

I inserted the key into the ignition and cranked the car. Full gas tank. Bless Brad for his kindness.

Dixie watched me closely from her position against the storage unit wall, a line between her eyebrows. Looked like she might be holding her breath, too.

Like an anxious mother hen with one chick. This is not how I wanted today to go.

"Are you standin' all the way against the wall 'cause you're scared I'm going to run over you?" I asked.

Death said the Gypsy Queen

"Well. It wouldn't be the first time, now would it?" Dixie retorted, noticing my teasing tone.

The statement startled a laugh out of me as I remembered those two teenage girls without a care in the world except for the freedom we'd just gained with our driver's licenses and a whole summer in front of us.

Foot firmly on the brake, I shifted the car into drive. "I was sixteen and had my license for about five minutes."

Dixie edged along the wall toward the exit. "All the same, let me get into my car before you start moving in this one." Dixie squinted in my direction, seemed satisfied by what she saw. "I'll stay right behind you all the way back to Mercy. And if you need to pull over, just do it and I'll pull in behind you."

I watched her saunter over to the Taurus parked next at the curb and get in. Still slender and quick as the teenage girl from that long ago summer. Taking a deep breath, I eased my foot off the brake and touched the accelerator gently.

CHAPTER TWO

Just before I pulled out onto the highway, I realized I hadn't put my Bluetooth device in my ear. The vintage Mustang looked like a dream, but it didn't have the modern day conveniences. Thank goodness, I'd remembered to bring the earpiece.

As I put the car back in park, I glanced in the rearview mirror and noticed Dixie's worried look. I rolled down the window and flashed her the OK sign. Once the earpiece was in place, I called her - just to make sure it was working right.

"Hey, girl. Nothing to worry about, I just realized at the last minute that I didn't have this earpiece in place and turned on."

"Thanks for letting me know. I was kinda worried about what's going on up there. I thought maybe you were having a prayer session before you get on the road."

I laughed. "That's actually a pretty good idea. But I'll keep it short so we can get on back home."

I disconnected the call; then sent up a prayer. *Lord. Please give me the strength to make this trip and make this change. Amen.*

As soon as I pulled out onto Highway 7 heading home, I felt sweat slick my palms as my knuckles went white on the steering wheel.

Death said the Gypsy Queen

It's only fifty miles. I whispered to myself. *Put your big girl panties on. You can do this. You have to do this. It's time.*

I hummed along with the radio to distract myself, and, when that didn't work, I sang out loud. That didn't seem to be helping either.

Keeping my eyes on the road, I rummaged blindly around the passenger seat with my right hand, but couldn't feel the phone. I hazarded a glance and saw that it had slid to the far side of the seat and dangled precariously on the edge.

"Hey Siri. Call Dixie." I said and the female computer voice told me it was calling Dixie.

I whooshed out the breath I'd been holding. Thank goodness for voice commands.

Dixie answered immediately, worry evident in her voice. "Are you okay? Should we pull over?"

I scanned the open countryside all around us. Cows to the left. Cows to the right. No emergency lane on this old country highway. Nowhere to pull over that would be safe at this point.

Besides, I was determined to try and make it all the way home anyway.

"I'm hell bent on getting over this fear of driving and it starts today. All that being said, I *am* feeling a bit nervous and I thought, maybe, if we talked it might help me calm down. Almost like you're sitting right here in the car with me."

"Sure." Dixie said agreeably. "So….what's going on with you and Vlad? Any chance of a romance budding there?"

Glad that Dixie couldn't see my beet red face, I answered. "Nunya, Dixie. Nunya."

Death said the Gypsy Queen

Dixie's laugh sounded good and I felt myself relaxing. This was the ticket. Something to keep my mind engaged.

"We'll get back to that one later, then. Hm. How about the secret genetics project Vlad is working on?"

I grimaced at myself in the rearview mirror, hoping Dixie could see it. "The operative word here is *secret*. I wasn't supposed to tell you about it at all."

Dixie sniffed. "Well, of course you told *me*. We're best friends our whole lives. I bet Vlad knew you'd tell me and he doesn't care."

Shifting in my seat a bit, I pushed away a feeling of guilt. But, Dixie was probably right. Vlad wouldn't care that the third of his only three childhood friends knew about the secret. But, still. "I thought we weren't going to talk about Vlad."

Dixie sighed. "We're *not* talking about Vlad. We're talking about his project up at the sleep study."

I stayed silent.

"I swear." Dixie said, after a full minute of silence. "You are the most pig-headed person in the world."

I did an eye roll even though no one could see me. Like being a bit stubborn was a bad thing? "And your point would be?"

When Dixie didn't respond, I went on. "I've been thinking I'm gonna do some genealogy research on the oldest families in town and trace where they came from and when they got here."

"And how is that not talkin' about Vlad's secret testing?" Dixie asked sarcastically.

Shouldn't that be perfectly obvious? "We're not talkin' about *Vlad's* project. We're talkin' about a *genealogy* project I'm planning to do."

"I hope you don't think I'm an idiot. You're planning to do the same thing Vlad's doing. Only you're gonna do it with old records instead of blood tests."

I thought that over for a minute. "You know what, Dixie? For someone who claims to be a dumb old country girl you sure are smart."

Dixie snorted. "I fix hair for a livin'. I hear it all from everybody. Kind of like a bartender. Only without the booze. You get to know folks pretty well that way. You get to where you can spot some bullshit when it's being shoveled."

I felt laughter bubbling up. "Are you saying I'm throwing some bull your way right now?"

"With all the bull you're shoveling back to me, it sounds like you're good to drive for a while." Then added in a smug voice, "Mission accomplished. Thank goodness. I need to plug my phone in to charge."

I looked around at the countryside and realized I had relaxed. No fluttering heartbeat. No sweaty palms. No feeling of impending doom. Maybe this was going to work out after all. There'd been nothing to be afraid of all this time.

Turning up the radio, I sang along with some of my favorite classic rock songs. The kind that were being recorded when this car was manufactured; and in the years that followed. I loved them for their robust, feel-good beat.

The miles rolls by. A black ribbon unrolling in front of me edged by leafy trees interspersed with rolling pastures dotted with cows.

Rolling down the window, I let the wind rush through the car and blow my hair around my face a bit, cooling me with its gentle touch. Laughing to myself, I stuck my hand out the window to wave at Dixie.

The car edged toward the ditch on the right. Just a tiny bit. Something no one else would think twice about. My blood ran cold.

I yanked my hand back inside and put it on the steering wheel. Feeling my heartbeat accelerate, I regretted the over exuberance that I'd let take over. One bad move and now my nerves were tight as guitar strings again.

Feeling panic building, I peeled my right hand off the steering wheel and reached over for my phone forgetting about using voice commands. Nevertheless, my hand shook so much that I couldn't keep pawing the passenger seat. I put the hand back on the wheel.

Okay. Calm down. You were perfectly fine a minute ago. Stop it. Stop it right now.

I couldn't get my brain to process the commands.

As though in answer to my silent fright, my phone rang with Dixie's ringtone.

ThankyousweetbabyJesus.

Reaching up with my still shaking hand, I managed to push the button that picked up the call on the earpiece on the second try.

"You need to pick up the pace up there, girl. We're pissing off a bunch of drivers behind us. Probably a bunch of college kids."

I hazarded a glance down to the speedometer. Forty. In a fifty-five. I silently cursed the two-lane highway. And my anxiety issues.

At that moment, a couple of horns blared from behind, scrambling my already stretched nerves, and I heard Dixie give a soft curse over the phone.

"Why the heck aren't these people back at the game?" Dixie wondered aloud.

"I'm pretty sure there's a rest stop just up the road. I'm gonna to pull off there. These people can go on by and I can rest for a minute."

Within a mile, I eased off the highway onto a paved parking area and pulled to a stop. Dixie rolled in beside me and a dozen cars blew past the entrance.

I hope you all get tickets. I mentally shouted at them and put my head down against the steering wheel.

A pecking sound on the glass next to me had me raising my head a moment later. Dixie motioned to me to unlock the door.

I opened it instead, got out and walked on wobbly legs to a picnic table nearby. Dixie went to her car, retrieved some bottled water and came back. Sitting next to me, she cracked the top on one and handed it over.

I smiled, took the bottle in both shaking hands to keep from splattering water all over the place and managed to swallow some cold water as I willed myself to calm down.

The coolness of the bottle felt good against my hands, so I pressed the bottle to my forehead in the hope of relieving the tension there.

"Thanks." I said to Dixie. "I'm not sure I could've opened it the way my hands are shaking."

"I hope y'all get fleas and can't reach 'em to scratch y'all dirty dogs!" Dixie shouted in the direction the cars had disappeared.

I smiled at the vision that created in my head.

"There." Dixie said. "That's better."

As I focused my eyes on Dixie, I saw something colorful at the edge of the rest area. Almost in the woods.

I leaned to the side to get a better look; and Dixie turned to see what had gotten my attention.

"Is that a gypsy wagon?" Dixie asked in an unbelieving voice.

CHAPTER THREE

"It sure looks like one," I answered. "But what's it doing out here?" I scanned the colorful wooden wagon sitting in a small clearing just barely in the tree line. Red with blue trim and a golden colored front door. Just right for wishes and dreams. It reminded me of some of the fairytales I'd been so fond of when I was a little girl. Was there an evil witch inside? Or a fairy godmother? I'd loved those stories back then.

Death said the Gypsy Queen

"And how did it get here?" Dixie wondered out-loud, dragging me back from my memories. "I don't see another car. Or even a horse."

I scanned the silent parking area. Hm. No one but us. No evidence anyone but us had been there recently. Of course, asphalt doesn't yield many clues, but you'd think if someone had been here there'd be a gum wrapper. Or a piece of trash. Something to indicate human habitation. Seeing as how people in general tend to be a messy bunch. Then there were the trees that edged right up to the pavement -- which was why I hadn't seen the wagon as soon as I'd pulled into the lot.

Well, that and the fact that I'd been on the verge of a full-blown panic attack.

I pushed that thought away to think over later. Right now, the gypsy wagon was entirely more interesting.

"Looks like it's got a trailer hitch on the front, so probably not pulled by a horse." I told Dixie. "Which still doesn't answer the question of how it got here. Unless whoever it belongs to left it here and took their car, or truck, somewhere else for some reason. Maybe they went to get something to eat. I'd hate to try maneuvering that thing in a restaurant parking lot or a drive through."

As we watched, the curtain on the front window twitched to the side and a gnarled hand motioned us to come closer. I felt Dixie slide closer to me and admitted, silently, to a bit of fright myself. These kind of things always happened in the scary movies I love so much. And I always holler at the girls to get up and get on out of there. But -- here I sat. Running not even entering my mind. I'd have to revise my hollering in the future.

"Do you think we've wandered into some kind of movie set up?" I questioned. "They've got that independent film community in Oxford."

"I don't see any cameras." Dixie answered, as her head swiveled side-to-side surveying the area. "Wouldn't there be cameras if there was some kind of filming going on?" She paused in her survey of the scene, eyes focused, and then pointed. "Oh lord. Is that a crystal ball on that table?"

I followed the pointing finger to see that a small table with a bright colored cloth full of embroidery sat a few feet away from the wagon. I stood up to get a better look, and, sure enough, there was a clear glass ball on it.

The hand in the window beckoned again.

A tiny shiver chased its way down my spine, but my curiosity sprinted out in front of any warning messages my intuition might be trying to convey at the moment.

"I'm going over there." I whispered.

Before I took two steps, Dixie grabbed my arm.

"Are you out of your mind?" She asked. "You could get kidnapped. Or murdered." Cutting her eyes over to the brightly colored wagon, she went on. "For all we know there's a couple of big, scary guys hiding in there just waiting for some unsuspecting women to walk into their trap."

I looked more closely at the wagon. It seemed so cute and inviting with its colorful paint and the little table off to the side. However, kids in fairy tales had been getting kidnapped for generations because they were taken in by some bright colors and friendly looking environments that turned out to be a bad choice. And there were always those girls in the scary movies I loved to watch. Their luck usually wasn't all that great either.

"I can't imagine what they'd want with a couple of middle-age chicks like us." I remarked with determination.

"Maybe not. But, how about that vintage mustang sittin' right over there? The one in showroom condition." Dixie asked with a raised eyebrow. "You don't think someone could get good money for it?"

I sat back down. Dixie *did* have a good point. As I vacillated between good sense and satisfying my curiosity, the door to the caravan creaked open and a short woman with gray hair bound back with a blue and red scarf stepped carefully down the steps holding her purple and green skirts high enough not to trip her; and revealing a pair of decidedly orthotic shoes. I pressed my lips together to keep from giggling and made it a point not to make eye contact with Dixie. If our eyes met, there'd be no holding back the laughter.

The woman gestured for us to come over, long fingernails painted as bright red as the mustang, and a collection of bangle bracelets jangling in the silence stretched between us.

Dixie's hand touched my arm, and then gripped it. "Don't you dare." She whispered in my ear. "Your nerves are shot to hell and back from driving and you're not thinkin' clearly right now."

That was surely the truth. But, the gypsy's eyes bore into mine with a hypnotic insistence. The desire to laugh over the shoes fled.

I stood up, shaking Dixie's hand off.

"I'm going over there. You stay here and if someone jumps out of that wagon and grabs me before I can run; you jump in the car and burn rubber out of here to get help."

Dixie's protest was no more than a buzzing sound in my ears as I covered the distance to the little chair in the shade. A breeze stirred the trees and allowed a shaft of sunlight to pierce through to the table, setting the crystal ball on fire with colors. From the pocket of her voluminous skirt, the gypsy produced a deck of oversized cards in the same bright colors as everything else associated with this little adventure.

Reaching the table, I sat in the wooden chair across from the woman, placing my hands in my lap.

The woman's hands shuffled the cards as her eyes bore into mine. Hers were so dark brown they were nearly black, the pupil almost invisible.

"I heard the curse your friend put on those travelers." She said into the silence in a hoarse voice.

"Curse!" I laughed nervously. "She didn't put a curse on anybody."

"She called out to the Universe to give fleas to those people."

"That's not a curse. She was just trying to make me laugh."

"You should always be careful what thoughts you put out into the Universe. It's always listening." The woman insisted. "She placed the deck of cards on the table between them. "Cut."

I shook my head. "I don't believe in all this."

"Of course you do. Otherwise you would have resisted the temptation and been on your way down the road by now." She glanced over my shoulder. "Your friend. She does not believe. But you do." She pointed to the deck of cards. "Cut."

"I don't even know your name." I said, trying to get a grip on my feeling of unreality. This woman was far too smooth an operator. Nothing like the fortune-tellers I'd met over the years at county fairs.

The woman gave me a knowing smile, revealing a set of perfectly white teeth.

Dentures? I wondered, still trying to make sense of my feelings.

"You may call me Angela."

"That doesn't sound very mysterious." I remarked, feeling a bit better.

Angela shrugged. "It is the name given to me by my mother."

Feeling a bit better after hearing the mundane name, I reached over, lifted the top third of the deck of cards and placed it to the side.

Angela reached over and picked up the cards I'd laid to the side, and showed me the card at the bottom.

Death.

My blood ran cold despite the heat of the Mississippi afternoon.

"Me?" I squeezed out the question past the constriction in my throat.

Angela shook her head. "Not you. But someone you know."

My heart slowed a bit, but not all the way to normal. Of course, that was not indicative of anything. It hadn't beat normally since I'd put the mustang in drive and pulled out onto the highway headed home to Mercy.

I chanced a look over my shoulder and saw Dixie sitting patiently at the picnic table, phone in hand, eyes glued to me. *Was she recording this whole meeting?* I waggled my fingers a bit hoping to reassure her.

Death said the Gypsy Queen

A stiff breeze washed across the open rest area and swept the Death card off the table onto the nearby asphalt where it whirled and tumbled along until Dixie slapped her foot on it.

I watched as Dixie bent and picked up the card. Her face registered shock when she saw the grim reaper representation and she got to her feet. Clutching the card, she walked stiffly to the table and held it out to Angela.

"I think this belongs to you."

Angela simply watched Dixie with quiet eyes rather than taking the card.

Dixie hand began shaking slightly. She laid the card face down on the table and turned to me.

"You 'bout done here? We need to get back on the road if you want to stop by the farmers market on the way back into town."

"Beware the vampire blood." Said Angela, then added. "It brings chaos and misery to you and yours."

My blood froze in my veins. How could this woman know about Vlad and the testing? Could she truly be in touch with some unseen force?

Dixie whirled on the woman. "Now look here." She said. "I don't know what your game is here, but I don't believe in all this woo-woo stuff you're preaching."

"The Universe. The stars. Call it what you wish. There are things only certain people can read from them. I am one of those people. Death will come soon."

Dixie yanked me from the chair, nearly pulling my arm from the socket. I barely got my feet under me in time to avoid falling to the ground. "Me and my friend aren't buying what you're selling so you can just stuff it with your universe and stars bologna." And dragged me back toward our cars.

I tried to pull my hand from Dixie's, but I'd've have had better luck pulling it from an iron vise. I looked back over my shoulder at Angela whose gaze seemed to plumb the depths of my soul before the other woman rose from her chair and went back into her caravan.

CHAPTER FOUR

"I told you that woman was on the take. Just waiting to get all of your money after she told you some cockamamie story." Dixie's voice nearly singed the hair from my head. Luckily, it was coming from the Bluetooth gadget in my ear and not face-to-face. And my anxiety about driving had been driven from my mind by recent events, pardon the pun, and I wasn't experiencing even a smidge of a tremor. More a sense of

amazement mixed with a healthy dose of
WTH.

We'd gotten into our cars and back
on the road as soon as Dixie had dragged
me to my car and opened the door for
me. I'd counted myself lucky she hadn't
shoved me into the seat and belted me
in.

Once we'd gotten a couple of miles
down the road, Dixie had called to
vent. I guess she couldn't hold off til
we got home.

"Actually," I replied. "You were
worried that some big scary guys were
going to carjack one, or both, of us as
I recall."

Dixie huffed out a breath over the
phone. "Don't distract me with details.
That woman is a fake and was about to
take your money."

"Well, seeing as how my purse was
in the car, I don't know how she was

going to pull that off. Besides, she never asked me for a dime."

"Exactly." Dixie replied in a huffy voice. "She saw me coming over there and knew she couldn't fool *me* with all her woo-woo sayings."

"How do you think she knew about Vlad's secret testing?" I asked.

"Please. That woman didn't know squat about squat. She was just throwing stuff out to see what reaction she got from you before she handed you some more of it. Why, from the look on your face when she said that about vampire blood, she knew she had you hook, line and sinker."

"But why would she say something about vampire blood? I mean, that doesn't sound like something that just anybody would buy into."

"I swear Lily Gayle Lambert. I don't know what has happened to your common sense. Where's the suspicious nature you usually have when it comes to things that don't make sense? If I didn't know better I'd think you believe her."

The mustang's tires sang on the asphalt as I considered that for a beat or two and then responded. "But why was she there? In that particular spot? And with no visible means of how she got there?"

Dixie snorted. "Come on, girl. You sound like you think she was waiting for *us*."

I let a few minutes pass as I thought everything over. Dixie had a point that there was no way the fortune-teller could have been waiting for us. Why, I hadn't known myself that I'd be pulling into that rest area until all that traffic had backed up behind us and made me more nervous than I'd already been.

Well, if she's really a fortune-teller with connections to forces you don't understand, then of course she knew you would stop there. Whispered a little voice in my head. I shook my head to clear the thoughts. This was doing nothing but going around in circles. Besides, there was no way in the world anyone could have predicted what Dixie and I were doing. Half the time we didn't know ourselves.

"You still there?" Dixie asked over the phone.

"Yep. Still here." I sighed. Then decided to mess with Dixie for the sheer entertainment factor. "I know it seems crazy, and you sure do have a valid point. But I can't help thinking we were meant to stop there and meet her."

"Have mercy." Dixie exclaimed. "We need to get you home and get your nerves back to normal 'cause I'm really concerned you've gone coo coo on me today."

"Don't be ridiculous. Can't I think there might be forces in this world beyond our understanding?"

"No. You can't. You've never thought that before in your life. And I'm not going to let you start it now."

"Fine." I responded. "Let's just agree to disagree on this one."

Some quiet muttering came over the phone. No doubt Dixie cussin' under her breath.

"What was that, hon?" I asked. "I can't quite hear you. Speak up."

"I *said* the farmers market is coming up and we were planning to stop there. Are you still up for it or do you need to go home and consult the stars before you make a move now?"

I smiled to myself. I'd sure gotten Dixie's goat. And provided myself with some more distractions on the drive home. The sign for the farmers market appeared on the right. Big red letters on a beige background with a big swooping arrow pointing to the turn.

"That's not what you were saying. I know you better than that." I turned on the blinker. "And we're going to stop just like we planned. I don't need a crystal ball to tell me I need some fresh vegetables to put up for later this winter."

Gravel popped under the mustang's tires as I cruised the length of the parking area looking for a spot. There was a big turn out today and I had to drive quite a ways back along the lot to find an open spot. It was coming up on the end of the season for a lot of vegetables. Local folks must be turning out to make sure they got what they wanted before it was gone.

Death said the Gypsy Queen

I'd already put up three dozen quarts of tomatoes this year. When they were at their peak. Not the stragglers that would probably be on sale now. Today I'd pick up butter beans and purple hull peas to do a quick blanch and freeze.

When I stood from the car seat, my legs trembled just for a moment. Like a sailor returning to land after a long trip at sea. I picked up each foot, shook it and set it back on the ground. After taking a few steps, I felt steadier on my feet. Just in time, too. Dixie strolled up just then, giving me a sharp look.

"You okay?" She gave me a quick once-over glance. "I'm talking about physically, 'cause we both know you're mentally unstable at this point."

Linking my arm through Dixie's, I laughed and pulled her forward. As we walked toward the entrance of the farmer's market, I said. "Okay. I confess. I was having a little bit of fun at your expense."

Dixie yanked her arm free, wheeled to face me and leaned into my face. "I oughta sock you right in the mouth. You had me worried to death and I couldn't do a thing about it."

I hugged my friend's unyielding body. "I'm sorry, Dix." When Dixie's body remained stiff, I hugged tighter. "Will you accept my apology? Please?"

Dixie pulled away, stuck her hands in her pockets and began walking again toward the entry gate. "I get that you were a nervous wreck. And that you were trying to distract yourself." She turned to look over her shoulder. "But do you get I was worried sick about you? Scared you were going to run in a ditch and hurt yourself?"

I halted. "You're absolutely right, Dixie. I wasn't thinking clearly. And that's my only excuse. Flimsy as it is."

Dixie stopped, turned slowly. "I really was worried about you getting hurt."

Regret washed over me. "Dixie. Please. I know I'm a pain in the rear sometimes. And I really am sorry. I swear."

"Well get a grip and stop acting like a spoiled kid." But she hugged me, accepting my apology.

CHAPTER FIVE

As we walked through the entrance area, I spotted Harley Ann Sanders at a booth she'd set up under a big oak tree. Customers were standing three deep and my heart swelled with pride.

Miss Edna's pretty, red-haired, great-niece had carved out a place for herself in Mercy. She'd been here less than a year. She'd come to live with Miss Edna after getting out of jail. She'd served several years for driving a get-away car for her boyfriend during a robbery. One she hadn't known they were committing until it was too late. Mercy was a new start for her and she was doing well.

We stopped to chat with Missy Elliott, the local real estate agent who was just leaving.

"How're Ian and Piper doing?" Dixie asked. "They went to Hawaii for their honeymoon, right?"

Missy smiled. "They sure did. They're having a great time, too. I promised Piper I'd look in on her daddy while they're gone so she wouldn't worry so much."

"I still can't believe that Mayor MacKenzie was an undercover informant for the FBI all those years without any of us suspecting." I grumbled.

Dixie laughed. "You're just mad that you didn't know yourself."

I frowned. "Just goes to show that you don't know what's goin' on in people's lives."

"I drive up to Memphis every day to visit him at The Med" Missy put in. "He's in really good hands and improving every day. Doing excellent when you consider he was shot so close to his heart." She smiled. "Thank goodness Ian had that old crop duster plane out at their barn so he could fly them straight to Memphis to the hospital."

"Piper's such a daddy's girl, I'm surprised she agreed to go on a honeymoon with him in the hospital and all." Dixie said.

Missy leaned in and spoke in a low voice. "That was all Ian's doing. And her daddy. And Ian's boss. A man named Hank Patterson who runs this Brotherhood Protectors group Ian works for now." She glanced around as though making sure no one was listening. "They all felt it would be best for Piper to leave the area for a while. They've put some agents on the Mayor's room at the hospital, so he's safe."

"Will Ian and Piper be living wherever it is that Ian's job has its home base?" I wondered.

"Eagle Rock, Montana. And, I honestly don't know." Missy answered. "I know Piper wants to stay close to her daddy and I don't see Matt MacKenzie ever leaving Mercy." She shook her head. "I'd love for them to live here myself. But, that's a decision for another day."

"Look." I touched Dixie on the arm to get her attention and motioned behind her. "They're stacked up over there wanting to buy some of Harley Ann's jams and flavored butters."

Dixie looked around as Missy held up a brown paper sack and said. "I've already gotten mine. I went to her booth first thing. Before she sold out of my favorites."

"Ooo! What'd you get?" Dixie asked, reaching for the bag.

Missy put it behind her back. "Oh no you don't. You'll have to go get your own."

I snatched the bag, dancing away from Missy as I opened it and looked inside.

"Lily Gayle Lambert!" Missy shouted in frustration. "Are you ever going to grow up?"

I handed her the bag. "Oh stop being such and old fuddy-duddy, Missy." I turned my eyes to Dixie. "She's got four jars of the bacon jam with the sippin' whiskey mixed into it in there."

Dixie narrowed her eyes. "Did you buy all of them she had?"

"I've got to run. I've got a showing in fifteen minutes." She hustled away from us, calling over her shoulder. "You two can get the flavors you want any time. The rest of us have to buy them when we get the chance."

I said to Dixie. "I reckon that means she *did* buy all of them that were available today."

Dixie sighed. "Dang it. I wanted to get some to put on my waffles in the mornings."

I linked arms with her and pulled in the direction of Harley Ann's booth. "Guess you'll have to use your connections and get some under the table."

The crowd thinned out a bit as we approached and I noticed Miss Edna coming from the opposite direction; make her way pretty well for an eighty-year-old with a walker.

The three of us arrived at the booth at the same time. Harley Ann hustled around the table to bring her great-aunt a chair to sit in.

"Thank you." Miss Edna said, sitting down with a sigh. "My old bones don't make such good time around this hard old ground out here."

Harley Ann handed her an open bottle of water. She sipped, then patted her lips with a lace hanky she pulled from her pocket.

Glancing at Dixie and me, she asked. "What have you two been up to this morning? You look a bit flushed Lily Gayle."

I felt my face flush some more and cursed inwardly. Why did she always have the ability to make me feel like a teenager who'd just been busted for lying?

"We rode down to Oxford and got Lily Gayle's car out of storage." Dixie supplied.

Miss Edna's eyes met mine. "Well done," was all she said. No sarcastic remarks.

I flushed even more at her rare praise.

"I was just talkin' to Mary Goodwyn over at her booth. She's got some late beans and pepper she's selling. She seemed to think she's going to beat me in the flower show next week. Silly woman. She should know by now that she can't be me."

"Her daughter, Sandra, is Elliott's favorite tech at their vet clinic." I said.

"What's that got to do with the price of tea in China?" Asked Miss Edna sarcastically.

And, just like that, all my benevolent feelings toward her vanished and things fell right back to normal in my world.

Dixie and I shared a look and rolled our eyes when Miss Edna glanced away, distracted by some shouting over by the cinderblock restrooms that had been built out here last year to make things convenient for folks buying and selling.

There was more shouting and heads started turning to see what all the ruckus was about. Just as I was about to suggest to Dixie that we go investigate, a woman's screams shattered the air and people stampeded over to the restrooms. Dixie and me right along with them leaving Miss Edna hollering for us to wait for her.

We shoved our way through the crowd and found Darla from the grocery store. Today, instead of smiling wide as she rang up groceries and chatted up customers, she was screaming the heavens down as a crowd of people stood frozen around her.

Dixie rushed up to the girl, talking in a soothing voice, trying to find out what all the commotion was about. When that didn't work, she hauled off and slapped Darla into next week.

The screaming stopped. The crying started.

Darla pointed into the corner where two walls met to offer a bit of privacy to those entering and exiting the ladies room.

Every eye on the scene followed the pointing finger. What we'd all missed while the screaming was going on was the body slumped onto the concrete pad. A wooden stake buried in the chest provided a big clue that the person didn't need emergency treatment. Blood trickled in a stream down the rough concrete and dripped onto the sun-scorched grass.

CHAPTER SIX

"Who is it?" Shouted a voice from the crowd and I unfroze myself. Glancing around, I couldn't determine who'd hollered. No one stood out as being more interested than the others. The group surged together as one, whispering among themselves and glancing around the area as though waiting for someone to do something.

I noticed Dixie hugging Darla and patting her back. She's got her hands full. Literally.

Death said the Gypsy Queen

I eased closer, trying to be careful not to disturb any evidence that might be lying around. But with so many people coming and going through here today, it's going to be tough to determine what's what.

"Everybody stay back." I said, ignoring the fact that no one was rushing to be of assistance. "And somebody call Ben."

I eased out in a semi-circle about ten feet from the crime scene, getting up on my tiptoes, squatting down, trying to make out who's laying there. I can see gray hair and a lanky body of a man, but that's about it. I can't identify the body from here.

I noticed Harley Ann and Miss Edna arrive at the edge of the crowd. Miss Edna looking fit to be tied at missing out on what's going on. I watched her point to me and motion Harley Ann to help her. Harley Ann gave me an apologetic look as she helped her great-aunt over the uneven ground to my side.

Miss Edna was breathing heavy by the time she got to me, but nothing was going to stop her so I didn't even comment. She braced herself on her walker, then squinted in the direction of the body.

She snapped her fingers at Harley Ann, and I wasn't even surprised when the girl pulled Miss Edna's "bird watching" binoculars from a big purse dangling from her shoulder.

Everyone watched us like a bunch of hawks. Waiting to see what happened next.

Miss Edna adjusted the binoculars. Took a look. Adjusted the binoculars again. I didn't know if she was really having trouble seeing the body or if she was just milking this for all she's worth. I wouldn't put it past her to be doing option two.

I heard a siren scream into the parking area back past all the tables and booths. Blue lights strobed around a few times before they shut off and Ben's deputy, Todd, got out of the car and started in our direction. He had his cellphone pressed to his ear and his mouth was moving. No doubt relaying everything to Ben.

"That's Larry Gordon!" Miss Edna shouted, drawing the attention of the crowd back to her. A buzz of conversation broke out immediately.

"Who?" I asked; puzzled that I didn't recognize the name. I'd grown up here after all. I'd been gone quite a few years, but the population of Mercy hadn't fluctuated much over the years.

I saw Dixie hand Darla off to her mama, who'd just arrived on the scene; and start over to Miss Edna and me. She kept her eyes on Todd, who'd put on crime scene gear before he approached the body. I hoped Dixie wasn't going to catch her foot in a low spot or hole and end up with a sprained ankle - or broken leg -- from rubbernecking and walking at the same time. She only glancing at the ground every few seconds to watch where she was stepping.

"I can't imagine who'd want to hurt poor, old Larry Gordon." She said when she reached us.

"You know him?" I questioned, wondering why I couldn't place the name.

Dixie nodded, reaching over to steady Miss Edna who'd stumbled a bit shifting her feet on the lumpy ground.

"You know him, too." She paused. When she saw I was still drawing a blank, she went on. "He ran the candy counter at the old Ben Franklin that used to be on the town square when we were kids."

I definitely remembered the old Ben Franklin store. We'd haunted that candy counter as kids. Carefully choosing our candy and counting out our pennies. Then taking our brown sack full of candy out to the lawn around the courthouse where we sat and ate candy til we were nearly sick. Back then, you could buy a sack full of candy for twenty-five cents. I sighed at the sweet memories. And, the face of the kind man behind the counter swam up from the depths of memory. He'd been old even then. But so kind and patient with a bunch of kids.

"I remember him now." I said. "I didn't know he was still around."

"He's been mostly a hermit for years." Miss Edna said. "But some of us older ladies who knew him when we were all children take him food from time to time and visit with him for a bit."

Her eyes misted over. "I can't for the life of me figure why anyone would want to kill him." The older woman straightened her back, standing tall. "I'm not gonna let anyone get away with this. The Triumphant Triumvirate will handle this case. Lily Gayle you get on over there with Todd and find out everything you can."

I was already reaching into my tote for the plastic booties and gloves I always carried around with me. I gave her a look.

"Don't get your back up with me, Lily Gayle Lambert. I am going to be part of this case no matter what you say or how you try to block me." She shook a wrinkled finger at me. "I know what you're thinking. I'm an old woman. I'm a pain in the tukhus. And, you're right. But that's neither here nor there. Get on over there and don't waste any more time."

Dixie gave me the stink eye from behind Miss Edna's back. No doubt she thought I'd protest some more, but I agreed with Miss Edna. Time was of the essence here. Besides, I didn't have time to be arguing about it right now.

I slipped on the plastic booties and rubber gloves under the amused gaze of the people still gathered to the side. Darla's mama had taken her somewhere. Not home, I hoped. I felt sure Ben was on his way here and would want to question her.

As I made my way over to the restroom building, Todd must have heard my booties on the dry grass because he looked up as I approached.

"Don't cover over here, Lily Gayle." He called.

I ignored him and kept right on walking. Much to the amusement of the audience. Snickers and giggles carried on the light breeze blowing through the site.

As I got to the edge of the concrete slab where Todd squatted next to the body, I thought I heard him say something under his breath about stubborn women and at least he'd covered his butt. No doubt thinking Ben would be angry when he saw me here.

I chose to ignore his muttering and squatted next to him.

"Miss Edna said this is Larry Gordon. Is that right?"

"Now Lily Gayle, you know I can't be giving you information on a criminal case."

I sighed. "Now, Todd. When have I not gotten information on recent cases I've helped Ben solve?"

His ears went bright red. I felt a flash of sympathy for him. His Mama'd taught him to have respect for his elders and here I was creating a problem for him. If I was committing a crime, I felt sure he'd be able to arrest me with no problem. But, since I wasn't committing a crime, he couldn't quite summon a level of command to tell me to get the heck out of the crime scene. Being a first cousin, and only living relative, of the county sheriff had its advantages, too.

The man who lay on the concrete slab definitely was old. His face sagged with wrinkles and his gray hair straggled across his head. I judged him to be about six feet tall when standing – which he wasn't right now. And, if I squinted, I could see the kind old man who'd helped me pick out my penny candy all those years ago. What could anyone have had against him?

Gravel popping in the distance told me another car had arrived. I'd bet all my money it was Ben. And that he'd be unhappy I was squatting here next to Todd. You'd think he would be used to it by now.

Sure enough, I heard the crowd shifting in the dry grass and looked over my shoulder. Yep. That was Ben. Dark look in his eyes and all.

He strode up, ignored me and directed all of his attention to Todd.

"What have we got here, Todd?"

Todd gulped, cut his eyes at me, and snapped them back to Ben when the sheriff cleared his throat.

"Uh. Right." And he shifted into cop mode. "Victim is Lawrence Donald Gordon. Age eight-two. Residence is 13056 Rodgers Creek Road, Mercy, Mississippi." He looked at Ben and said. "Why would anyone kill an old man like this?"

Ben shook his head. I could see memories flashing through his mind. Probably some of the same that had flashed through mine. Ben had been among the group of kids that Larry Gordon had helped with their candy. He squatted next to us.

"I don't know, Todd. That's one we'll have to figure out." He glanced around at the crowd still watching us. "Does anyone know if Larry Gordon has any living family members?"

The onlookers glanced at each other, but no one volunteered any information. So, either there weren't any family members. Or someone who had information didn't want to get involved. At least not out here in front of anybody.

I racked my brain trying to pull up any information on the Gordon family I might have come across in my years of doing genealogy searches. Nothing came to mind. But, that didn't mean there wasn't any information there. I'd check my records when I got back home. Maybe

I'd turn up something that might help
with the case. Or, at least with laying
Larry Gordon to rest with some
ceremony.

CHAPTER SEVEN

I drove home from the farmers market without a single nervous twitch. Maybe that was the trick to my driving issues. Have something distracting on my mind when driving. I could see that being a problem in itself though. Distracted driving is dangerous.

Dixie pulled into the drive right behind me. She'd followed me this time because she wanted to know what I found out about the Gordon family from my notes more than that she felt like I needed the support of knowing she was right behind me.

I pulled my laptop from the side table drawer where I kept it and turned it on. "Would you mind getting us a couple of glasses of sweet tea while I'm getting the program open?" I asked Dixie.

She nodded and headed down the short hallway to the kitchen. The house had an unusual layout. My grandparents had built it over a hundred years ago and house plans were a lot different back then. I heard a cabinet slam in the kitchen as Dixie rummaged around in there. I didn't think she'd done it on purpose until she marched into the living room with two jars in her hands. Harley Ann's Whiskey Bacon Jam. I'd been hiding them.

"So. You know I've been out of this for two months and yet you don't offer up one of your own jars?" She asked, one eyebrow quirked upward.

Oops! The Whiskey Bacon Jam was Harley Ann's hottest selling product. Chunky, sweet and salty bacon and onion with a bit of Tennessee sippin' whiskey added to give it a subtle kick. Cooked down to a thick spreadable paste. I didn't know what else was in there since Harley Ann wouldn't share the recipe for love or money. And, she couldn't produce enough to meet demand.

As evidenced by Missy Elliott buying four jars at the farmers market this morning. Now *that* was downright selfish if you asked me. Harley Ann should put a limit on how many jars a person could buy at one time since it was such a hot product. I'd had mine for a while and used it sparingly to make it last as long as possible.

"Those are the one I bought when you were with me." I told Dixie. "You bought three jars at the same time I did. Is it my fault you ate all of yours already?"

Dixie gave me her sad face and I relented. "Oh, for Heaven's sake. You can have one jar."

She tucked it into her purse immediately and I smiled. She really did love that stuff.

"Okay." I said. "Here's my list of notes on families in Mercy." I scanned over the list and found the name Gordon. Good. I'd done some research on the family at some point.

"Don't you think it's really odd that Larry Gordon was murdered with a stake through his heart?" I asked Dixie.

"Well, sure. It's not like you see something like that every day."

I waited. But that was it. I sighed. "Seriously? That's all you've got? Especially after that woman told us to beware the vampire blood not an hour before he was found? Hello? Vampire blood? Stake through the heart?"

"Don't be silly." Dixie said. "That woman was a fake. There's no way she had any knowledge of this murder…unless she's involved in some way." Dixie grabbed her phone out of her purse.

"Who are you calling?"

"Ben."

"What for?"

"Because we need to tell him about that woman. What she said about vampire blood. She could be involved with whoever murdered poor old Larry Gordon."

"I promise you. There's no need to call him. He'll be over here in no time telling me to stay out of his business." I heard gravel popping in the driveway. "That's probably him now."

Dixie glanced out the window. "Nope. It's Harley Ann and Miss Edna."

I groaned. "I was hoping she wouldn't stick her nose in this one."

Dixie laugh. "Kind of like Ben hopes *you'll* keep your nose out of it?"

I glared at her. "That's entirely different."

A knock on the door distracted us, and Dixie went to answer it.

Miss Edna stumped into the room with her walker, Harley Ann close behind. Still looking apologetic. That girl needed to get some gumption. I knew she was grateful to her great-aunt for giving her a home, but that was no reason to let the old woman run all over her. I sighed inwardly. That was a subject for another time.

"What have you come up with, Lily Gayle?" Miss Edna asked, settling herself in a club chair that sank low even with her light weight and sucked her backward into the stuffing. I managed to hold in my laugh as the older woman struggled to pull herself to the edge of the chair and balance there.

"Let me get you a kitchen chair, Miss Edna." Dixie said. "Those overstuffed chairs are worse than a feather mattress for sinking you down so far you can't see daylight."

Dixie was back in a flash with the wooden chair and Miss Edna shifted herself over to it. Once she'd settled herself, her attention turned back to me.

"Well? Cat got your tongue, girl?"

At my blank look, she pounded her fist on the frame of her walker.

"For Lord's sake, girl! What have you found on the Gordon's in your files? I just know you've gotten information on them in all the research you've done over the years."

I resisted the urge to strangle the cantankerous woman. She was only saying the same thing I'd been talking to Dixie about before we got distracted.

"I was just pulling up the information I have when you got here. I don't remember working on it, so the information is probably pretty old."

Miss Edna waved a dismissive hand. "Nothing to worry about. I can tell you poor old Larry never got married. His true love married someone else and moved away. Broke his heart."

"In that case, the information I have may be all there is." I clicked on the file labeled Gordon. The date on the file was seven years old. I glanced through the skimpy information trying to find anything that might be interesting here and now.

"Well?" Asked Miss Edna. "Don't keep us sittin' here like bumps on a log. What've you got?"

Dixie crossed her eyes behind Miss Edna's back, making me grin.

"What so amusing?" Miss Edna squinted at me. "Are you making fun of me? Your mama taught you better than to make fun of your elders. She'll be rolling in her grave."

"There's not much here." I told her. "The file is seven years old. All it has is the original family members who settled here and their descendants. Nothing other than names and what part of the county they lived in."

"Nothing about *where* they came from?" Miss Edna inquired pointedly. "Or who they live next to or may be related to? The Mitchells, maybe? Or…the Templetons?"

"I can't conjure up information, Miss Edna" I told her, struggling to hide my dismay at her direct questions. "There's nothing here that gives me that information."

"Hmph. Do you take me for a fool, missy?"

"Well, I don't know what it is that you think I'm holdin' back, Miss Edna." I summoned my best wounded look to make my statement more convincing.

"Larry had a wooden stake through his heart." Miss Edna said. "I saw it with my binoculars."

I glanced at Dixie who shrugged. Dang it. Miss Edna was going in the direction I meant to explore on my own. Without her interference.

"Yes." I answered. "I saw that close up when I went to talk with Todd." I shuddered. "Pretty gruesome."

"Harley Ann, help me up from this chair." Miss Edna struggled to get to her feet before her great-niece could get to her. She pointed a shaking finger at me.

"Now you listen here, Lily Gayle.

You aren't fooling me for one single minute with that delicate female act you just put on. I know when I'm being hornswoggled and you're trying to do it to me. I don't appreciate it at all. I'm part of this investigation team and you best stop trying to withhold information from me."

She started toward me with her walker and I wondered for a minute if she planned to brain me with it when she got close enough. We were spared from finding out by gravel popping out in the driveway.

Dixie jumped up from her chair and looked out the window. "It's Ben."

"About time." Miss Edna said, moving back to her chair and sitting down. "Now we'll get some information."

I laughed. "If you think Ben's here to give us the scoop on the investigation, you're very mistaken. You know as well as I do that he's here to tell us, me especially, to keep out of the case."

Miss Edna sniffed. "Since when has that ever stopped you? Or us?"

I heard Ben's shoes on the wooden boards of the front porch, then the front door opened. He never knocked. He always said family doesn't have to knock. So far he hadn't walked in on anything either one of us regretted. I don't know if that means I live a very boring life or not.

His eyes took in the gathering in my living room and he sighed. But why he did, I didn't know. He must've known who was here by the cars parked in my driveway.

"'Bout time you got here." Miss Edna said. "Lily Gayle is tryin' her best to cut me out of the case and I'm not going to let her do it." She settled back more comfortably on her chair.

"Now, you go right on and tell us what's going on so far."

Ben shook his head. "You do take the cake, Miss Edna. You know I don't appreciate y'all gettin' mixed up in my cases."

"Is that right?" She said sarcastically. "Seems to me we've helped you solve several of them lately."

I secretly cheered at her words, but outwardly kept my cool. No use setting Ben off on a rant if we could avoid it. Honey catches more flies than vinegar. I'd've thought an old southern belle like Miss Edna would've had that saying embroidered somewhere.

"Now, Miss Edna. We've just been some help to Ben. We haven't taken over the cases at all."

Miss Edna and Ben both shot me astonished looks. I couldn't blame them. I guess I had laid it on a bit thick.

I cleared my throat. "What I mean to say is that we don't mean to take over your cases, Ben. It just seems to work out sometimes that we come up with some significant pieces of information."

Ben ran his hand through his hair. "You can stop with the B.S., Lily Gayle. We both know you interfere and cause problems all along the way." He scanned the others in the room. "Along with your sidekicks here."

I stood up, but Ben held up a hand to stop me saying anything. "I came by to ask you if you know where Vlad Templeton is. I went up to the Midnight Dragonfly to talk to him, but the assistants there told me he'd gone out of town. And he's not answering his phone."

Dixie and Harley Ann gasped. Miss

Edna cackled.

"I knew there was some connection to either the Mitchells or the Templetons." She said.

"Oh for heaven's sake, Miss Edna." I said in exasperation. "How could you know that?"

"I've heard a couple of rumors lately that there's more going on up there than a sleep study." She answered with a smug grin.

Vlad Templeton had left Mercy, Mississippi as a child and come back last year with a government funded sleep study in his back pocket. He'd set up the study at the old Mitchell manor on the hill outside of town. After the Mitchell's had all died or ended up in jail, the place had been refurbished into a bed and breakfast called the Midnight Dragonfly. Vlad had taken over the house for his sleep apnea study funded by the state.

But Ben, Dixie and I knew that he was also conducting secret DNA tests on the townspeople, trying to determine who might have a genetic anomaly that caused hypertrichosis, also known as wolfman syndrome. And another genetic anomaly that caused porphyria, also known as vampire syndrome. Ben had investigated when we found out about the secret studies and confirmed Vlad's claim that it wasn't against the law in Mississippi to do secret DNA testing.

The Mitchell family and the Templeton family were both positive for the anomalies. Vlad was looking for more people who had it and didn't know about it to help him come up with treatments for them.

Ben and I exchanged looks at Miss Edna's pointed questions. I didn't dare look at Dixie.

"You want to tell me about these rumors?" Ben asked.

Death said the Gypsy Queen

"I can tell from the way you two just looked at each other that you already know what I'm talking about." She replied with a frown. Like a child who'd been hoarding a secret only to discover it wasn't a secret after all.

"All the same." Ben answered. "If you believe the rumors you've heard have a connection to this case, you need to let me know what they are. And who you heard them from."

Miss Edna carefully adjusted the skirt of her dress as though it was the most important thing in the world. I could tell she was deciding how much to tell Ben. And maybe regretted saying as much as she already had.

"Well, Sheriff. Rumor has it that Vlad Templeton's testing people for vampire blood. Or even wolfman blood."

Ben grimaced. As well he might. Miss Edna's words struck a nerve for both of us. Vlad's secret was out. And making its way silently underground through the town.

"Well, I reckon I'll take that under consideration, Miss Edna. But there's nothing for you to be worried about."

Miss Edna let out a cackling laugh. "I'm not worried about a thing, Sheriff. *My* family isn't one of the old ones around here." She paused, looking around the room at all of us in turn. "And I know all y'all know what I mean by *that*."

She motioned to her great-niece. "Help me out to the car, Harley Ann. We're done here for now." She glanced at Ben. "If you want to talk to me some more, Sheriff. You know where I live." She glanced back from the front door. "And I'll expect an update on the case from you, Lily Gayle. Once you've gotten some new information."

Dixie, Ben and I watched as Harley

Ann helped her great-aunt out to the car and drove off.

"Well. That sure takes the cake." I said.

"Sounds like Vlad's in some trouble." Dixie added.

Ben shifted his gun belt, resettling it around his waist. "I didn't realize rumor was running rampant around town. That makes it even more imperative I get in touch with him."

"I don't think rumor is running rampant just yet." Dixie said. "I'd've heard it at the beauty shop if it was. And, so far, not a whisper."

"Well. Thank goodness for small favors." Ben answered. He turned to me. "I've got to go and check on some things right now. Doc Johnson is going to do the autopsy tomorrow morning. You meet me there and we'll go in together.

Well knock me over with a feather.

CHAPTER EIGHT

Bright and early the next morning, I pulled into the parking lot on the back side of the hospital where the morgue is located in Mercy. I put the mustang in park and wallowed in the sense of accomplishment for a minute. For most people, driving a couple of miles in a quiet country town was nothing. For me, it was a new beginning.

As I headed to the door, I glanced around for the sheriff's department car

Death said the Gypsy Queen

Ben usually drove when he was on the clock, but didn't see it. Guess that meant I'd have to deal with my nemesis, Jimmy John Spencer, on my own. Unless I wanted to wait around out here til Ben showed up.

Riding high on my successful drive, I decided to face down Jimmy John. We'd never liked each other in our entire lives. You'd think we'd've outgrown it, but it hadn't happened. We still couldn't see eye-to-eye on anything. Today wouldn't be the first time we'd crossed swords over me being here for an autopsy. He liked to throw his weight around as the keeper of who got past him to the autopsy suite and Doc Johnson.

I opened the door, walked in and faced his frown with a big smile of my own.

"Good morning, Jimmy John. I'm here to meet the sheriff and attend the autopsy of the guy that got murdered yesterday."

Jimmy John gave me a sour look. He rifled through some papers on his desk and made a big deal out of clicking around on his computer. "I don't have any notice of permission that you're going to be here today. So you sit right on down in one of these here chairs until either the sheriff or the doc shows up to let me know you're not trying to pull a fast one."

I sat down with a big smile on my face and a show of good grace while inside I seethed. He knew darn good and well that either one of those men would walk me straight back the minute they got here. I took some small pleasure in the disappointed look on his face right now. Guess he thought I'd kick up a big fuss – I certainly had in the past. But, today, I wasn't in the mood.

Luckily, Ben strode through the

door within five minutes. I might not have been able to keep my good mood if I'd had to deal with Jimmy John for an extended period.

"Hey, JJ!" Ben said. They'd played football together in high school and stayed friends all these years. "Lily Gayle giving you a hard time this morning?"

I jumped up to defend myself, but, surprisingly, Jimmy John grinned at Ben. "Nope. She's mindin' her manners this time."

Well that just made my blood boil. But before I could launch into either of them, Ben said.

"Let's head on back. The doc should already be back there and ready for us."

And, just like that, we walked past the guard dog.

As we walked along the linoleum-covered hallway to the autopsy suite at the back, Ben said, "I don't know why you can't be nice to him all the time. It makes it easier to deal with him. You know he's a blowhard anyway."

I ran my fingers along the green cinderblock wall as I thought over my reply. Ben had a point about being nice to Jimmy John. But, he just pushed all of my buttons without even trying. I knew it was wrong and childish, but could rarely prevent myself from locking horns with him.

Ben glanced over at me. "Hard head."

I laughed. "Some things never change."

We pushed through the double doors to the autopsy suite to find Doc Johnson making notes on a chart. I was relieve to see he'd already made the Y incision and saved me from watching that.

The doc looked up from a clipboard

in his hand. His still handsome face held sadness.

"Ben. Lily Gayle. I'm glad y'all are here." He placed the chart in a metal holder. "I've got some interesting findings to tell y'all about. First, take a look here." He pointed at the neck.

I leaned over to see what he was pointing to. Poor old Larry had a 'chicken neck' that a lot of old people get. At least the skinny ones do. I squinted; trying to make out what Doc wanted me to see. At last, I noticed some small round scabs among the wrinkles.

"The scabs?" I asked to make sure.

"Yep." Doc looked at Ben. "You see them, too, Sheriff?"

Ben nodded looking as confused as I felt. What did those have to do with the stake through his heart?

As though reading my mind, Doc

flapped his hands at me. "I know. I know. But, have a bit of patience, please."

I nodded.

"I found these round puncture marks that are scabbed over. But I also found some round puncture marks that are healed up. Like they've been there for a while. And there were several of them. Always two holes. Parallel to each other and approximately an inch and a half apart."

He watched us with expectant eyes.

Ben and I glanced at each other.

"Do you mean like a dog bite?" Ben asked.

"Very similar." Doc answered.

"On his *neck*?" Ben questioned.

Doc nodded, still with the expectant look on his face.

It suddenly dawned on me what Doc wanted us to put together.

"Like a *vampire* bite!" I exclaimed.

"Well. Probably not a vampire. Don't know that I believe they actually exist." Doc said. "But more likely human than canine based on the distance between the teeth."

"Some of the bigger dog breeds have teeth pretty far apart." Ben put in.

"True." Doc conceded. "But, in my opinion, a large dog would have caused a lot more damage than just a couple of puncture wounds. I believe there'd be some tearing of the skin."

Doc jumped at us and we both jumped backward.

"You see?" He said. "If you're being attacked by something big, your natural instinct is to jump backward. If a big dog had gotten its teeth into his neck, I think there would be more tearing to the skin."

"You said there were old scars that look like healed tooth marks?" I asked.

Doc nodded.

"So you think whatever caused this has been going on for a while?"

Doc nodded.

"Do you think one, or more, people have been playing at vampire games?" I asked.

Ben shot me a disgusted look, but Doc nodded.

:"That's exactly what I think has been going on." He looked sadly at the man on the table. "I just wonder if they got tired of playing the game and decided to get rid of him in a way that they thought would be permanent."

He picked up a clear plastic bag holding a piece of wood from the table next to him. Dark gray, about twelve inches long and sanded or honed some other way into a dagger shape. "This is the murder weapon. But y'all saw it out at the farmer's market when the body was found."

"How is it possible for a piece of wood to be sharp enough to penetrate clothing and skin and go all the way to the heart?" I asked.

"And how hard is it to actually hit the heart?" Ben questioned. "As opposed to just stabbing someone in general. Was it a fluke that the stake actually hit the heart?"

Doc looked pleased. Like a professor with two eager students.

"Those are excellent questions." He smiled. "Just the kind I'd expect from our sheriff and his intrepid cousin."

I felt a blush crawl up my cheeks at the praise even as I noticed Ben's less than happy look.

Doc held the plastic bag containing the stake out toward the two of us so we could see better. "If you look closely, you'll see a dark gray metal tip on the end of the wood. It's razor sharp. Very handy for penetrating clothing and skin. And Ben, this stake is actually slender enough to have passed between the ribs and hit the heart. I couldn't say if it was a lucky strike or one from knowledge of anatomy."

"Doc, do you think the wooden stake is significant to the murder? Like the silver bullet when the wolf man was killed two years ago?" I asked.

"That's for the two of you to figure out."

He sighed and laid the bag back on the table next to him. "There nothing else of note to tell you at this point. He was in pretty good shape for an eighty-two year old man. A bit malnourished, but nothing life threatening. He should have had some more years left."

As Ben and I exited the building, after I'd given Jimmy John the stink eye on the way past his desk, Ben said, "I suppose it's too much to ask you to keep your nose out of the case."

"You suppose right." I answered. "And you know it. Otherwise you'd never have invited me to the autopsy this morning."

Ben shook his head. "A man can hope."

CHAPTER NINE

Dixie's Taurus sat in the driveway when I pulled in, with Ben right behind me. I'd called her on the way home and asked her to meet us at the house. Ben wanted to go over everything we'd seen yesterday morning. Even though I told him, we didn't know anything.

I remembered on the drive home I'd never told him about the fortune-teller Dixie and I had met on the way home from Oxford. I could already hear

Dixie's opinion about that. However, Ben needed to know about it anyway.

I hopped out of the car and spotted Dixie in one of the wicker rockers on the porch. Elliott, my fat and sassy Maine Coon cat, sat perched in her lap. Poor kitty. I guess he was feeling a bit neglected this morning.

"Hey, girl!" I hollered as Ben and I walked toward the house.

Dixie put Elliott on the porch with a final pat and stood up to meet us as we came up the steps.

"I don't know what y'all think I can contribute to this conversation. I don't know anything." She said, echoing the words I'd give to Ben earlier.

"Actually, I realized we forget to tell Ben about the fortune-teller yesterday."

Dixie rolled her eyes. "You got me over here for *that*? I hope you realize I'm gonna have to leave shortly. I've got a customer coming to the shop in an hour for color. And you know that's one that takes some prep, so let's get a move on."

"What fortune-teller?" Ben asked. "I didn't know they had one at the farmer's market."

I unlocked the front door and the three of us went to the kitchen. Ben and Dixie sat at the big round table by the window overlooking the woods out back as I got glasses down from the cabinet and put ice in them to pour us some sweet tea.

"There's not a fortune-teller at the farmer's market." I said as I got the tea out of the refrigerator and began pouring it into the glasses. "We met her at that rest stop about ten miles out Highway 7 going toward Oxford."

Ben wrinkled his forehead. "As I recall, there's nothing there but some asphalt."

"You're right." I said, setting the glasses of tea on the table and taking a seat myself. "I was kind of nervous driving home."

I ignored his sharp look of concern. He'd wanted to be the one to go to Oxford with me and get the mustang. But I'd vetoed that idea knowing it would've made me far more nervous for him to be the one following me. I deliberately left out the part about backing up all that traffic. He didn't need to know the details.

"So, we pulled in there to let me take a breather. And, while we were sittin' at that one table that's out there, I noticed this brightly painted wagon. Almost back in the trees. And with a little table next to it."

"I was the one that noticed the crystal ball on the table." Dixie put in.

"*Crystal ball*?" Ben repeated in disbelief. "Y'all should've got in the cars right that minute and headed on back here. No good can come from some random fortune-teller wagon set up on the side of the road."

Dixie gave me her *told you so* look. Which I ignored.

"Anyway. Cuttin' to the chase, here." I glared at Dixie. "The woman told me to beware the vampire blood."

Ben stood up so fast his chair flipped over backwards. "What the *hell*?"

"I know." I said. "In light of what happened when we got to the farmer's market it seems more significant than it did at the time she said it."

"She thought the woman was talking about Vlad's secret testing." Dixie added.

Ben picked up his chair, turned

it and straddled it, resting his arms across the back as he glanced at each of us. "I need to find that woman. She may have been involved somehow in the murder." He ran a hand through his hair, then blew out a breath. "She's probably long gone by now, though. Dammit! I wish y'all had mentioned this yesterday."

He pulled his phone from his pocket. Chose a number and placed it against his hear. "Yeah. Todd. I need you to run out Highway 7 toward Oxford to the rest stop out there. See if you can find a woman in a bright colored fortune-teller wagon."

I heard a questioning voice on the other end.

"Yes. I said fortune-teller wagon. Get on out there now and call me back when you have any information."

He disconnected the call and put the phone back in his pocket. "I hate to send Todd on a wild goose chase. The woman is probably gone. But on the off chance she's not, we need to bring her in for questioning."

Dixie drained her tea and set the glass back on the table. "Well this has been more fun than I can handle and I've got a customer to get to."

She stood. "Y'all let me know what else happens." She added. "Don't forget you have an appointment tomorrow, Lily Gayle."

Ben stood as well. "I'm gonna go on out to that rest stop and look around myself. Maybe there's something out there."

I saw them both to the door, and when it was shut, sat down in my favorite chair to think over all the activity from the past two days.

As I tried to get everything straight in my mind, the landline phone rang scaring me out of ten years

growth. Hardly anybody calls me on it
and most of the time I forget it's
there. I don't know why I haven't just
disconnected the thing.

I reached over and picked up.
"Hello?"

"I know about that secret testing
going on up to the Midnight Dragonfly."
Said a muffled voice that I thought was
female, but couldn't be positive.

My pulse picked up at the words
and the unexpected message and voice.
Creepy.

"Who is this?" I asked in a calm
voice that belied my agitation. "I'm
not in the mood for silly games."

"You need to get on up to the
Dragonfly and warn Vlad he's in deep
trouble. Get him to leave town if you
can."

A dial tone sounded in my ear.

I placed the receiver carefully
back on the cradle, wondering if the

whole world knew about Vlad's secret tests. Didn't seem to be much secrecy to them. At this rate, I reckon there'll be an article in the Argus next week all about it.

Since Ben had already told us that Vlad was out of town, I decided to see if I could catch him on his cell phone. He might be answering by now. Maybe he'd been avoiding call from Ben for some reason and would pick up if he saw it was me. Either way, I needed to find out if he could be reached. I'd leave him a voice message warning if he didn't answer.

I lucked out and he picked up on the first ring.

"Vlad. Where are you?" I asked without any of the usual pleasantries.

"I'm almost back to Mercy. I had a voicemail from Ben about some murder there that he thinks might have a connection to my tests. I didn't call him back. I was done with my meeting so I jumped in the car and headed home. I figured a face-to-face talk would be better than on the phone."

"Well hold on to your britches because I'm about to add to your troubles."

I explained about Larry Gordon and then added the information about the anonymous call I'd just gotten.

"Larry Gordon was one of my patients during the early days of testing. Even though he doesn't have any living relatives in town I wanted to test him because he's from one of the oldest families." He lowered his voice, like someone might hear him. "You know why that interested me."

"That's some information Ben will surely want to know about." I thought I heard something out on the porch, but when I peeked around the edge of the curtains, I didn't see anything in the moonlight-flooded yard or on my porch.

Vlad gave a quiet curse over the phone. "This is a stroke of really bad luck that word seems to have gotten out about the secret testing. I can't imagine how that happened unless it was one of my employees. And they all signed an agreement that anything they see or learn at the study is top secret."

"Yes. I believe it's going to cause you some trouble from here on out. If it's one of your employees, maybe they think that the paper they signed doesn't pertain to the secret tests you didn't tell them you were conducting? Maybe you should hold off on them now that word is getting out and people seem to be upset about it."

"I can't stop the tests. I'm close to some incredible information. So incredible that I can't tell even you, Lily Gayle."

That chapped my hide a bit, but I could understand. Top-secret scientific stuff should be kept top secret. Even though it looked like he had a big leak already.

"Don't worry. I get it." I told him. "Call me tomorrow and let's get together. It'll probably have to be after Ben gets done questioning you. And if he doesn't throw you in jail."

"I hope you're joking. Because, if you're not, I'm not going to let anyone know I'm back. There are places in that house I can hide where no one can find me. Not even you."

I remembered the secret passageway Dixie and I had discovered at the Midnight Dragonfly. The one that had helped us save a couple of lives; and knew he was probably right. He'd spent several years there as a child and had no doubt found all kinds of interesting secrets there.

"Oh. One more thing. I almost forgot to tell you." I said before he could disconnect. "There was this strange fortune-teller woman at the rest stop outside of town that told me to beware the vampire blood. Pretty crazy, huh?"

Silence. I wondered if we'd gotten disconnected. Maybe he was driving through a dead zone. There were quite a few in this area.

"Hello?" I said again. No answer. He must be in one of those zones.

CHAPTER TEN

I arrived at the It'll Grow Back, Dixie's hair salon on the square in Mercy, to find it busting at the seams with ladies – all of them yelling. It looked like a lot of talking and not much listening as every one of them was trying to get her personal story or opinion told and didn't give a darn who was actually listening.

They were all waving around pieces of white paper. I grabbed one out of Jenny Ayle's hand to see what all the shoutin' was about.

My blood ran cold when I read the words.

Someone had printed out a warning that Vlad Templeton was conducing secret DNA tests at the Midnight Dragonfly Sleep Study to find out which residents of Mercy were carriers of vampire blood. And, possibly of wolf man blood. It also referenced the dead wolf man case from two years ago and the connection to the Mitchell family that used to own the house where the Midnight Dragonfly Sleep Study was being conducted.

I glanced around trying to locate Dixie in all the squirming bodies. I didn't see her, so I pushed through the crowd to the back of the shop where Dixie had a small office to keep her records and store extra products. She was in there, on her phone, shouting at someone.

"I don't care if there's a wreck out on the interstate and all y'all are out there trying to help with it. I need one of you to get your butt over here to my shop before these crazy women destroy the place. They're all mad enough to eat fire and spit nails."

I quirked an eyebrow at her.

Ben. She mouthed back.

"Ben Carter. If you don't get over here and take care of this I'm gonna start shootin' to silence them. I won't mean to hit anybody, but there's so much going on that someone might accidentally get shot."

She paused. Listened.

"*No.* I don't want you to send Todd over here. He'll be worse than useless with this bunch. Hello? Hello?"

She screamed and threw the phone forcefully into the closet where she stored towels. It hit the stack of towels and bounced to the floor.

"He hung up on me. What am I supposed to do about that riot going on out there? Are they destroying my property?"

I shook my head. "I didn't see any destruction going on. But, there's a bunch of pissed off women out there. All shoutin' at the same time. I couldn't hear myself think it was so noisy."

She reached into the back of her desk drawer and pulled out a Glock. I boggled over the sight of it. Dixie'd always been such a pacifist that I'd thought she was kidding about shooting up the place.

"Now, Dixie." I cautioned.

She shot me a harassed look and went to the door leading back out into the shop. Putting two fingers of her left hand to her mouth, she let out a whistle that nearly deafened me in the tiny back room. I heard the commotion out in the shop die back a little bit. But it started right back up.

I tried to grab her arm when I saw her raising the gun. Not the smartest move on my part. If she squeezed the trigger trying to pull her arm away from me, she might shoot somebody out in the shop. Or one of us.

She shifted away from me, raised the gun straight up and pulled the trigger. The sound was deafening. And had an immediate effect. Every woman in the room stopped talking, but had her mouth hanging open. Not one of them would have bet Dixie Newsom owned a gun. Or that she'd actually shoot it.

Right then, Ben pulled up out front in the squad car and all of the ladies rushed outside and confronted him, waving the papers overhead. I saw him take one, read it and frown.

I edged up to the front door and cracked it open enough to hear what was being said. They were shouting about illegal testing. Ben told them it wasn't illegal in Mississippi to conduct the DNA testing Vlad was doing. And *that* set them off even more. That he'd known about the testing long enough that he'd researched the legality of it stuck in their craw. It was his job to protect this town and the people in it and they clearly felt like he hadn't done that.

His shoulders slumped at that accusation. I knew it hit him hard to hear that. And no amount of telling him that the people were scared and didn't mean it would change a thing at this point.

"What about Larry Gordon?" Someone shouted. I looked in the direction the voice had come from. Sandra Goodwyn. Elliott's favorite vet tech.

She hollered out. "Was he a vampire? Is that why he got killed like that? With the stake through his heart?"

"Somebody needs to go up to that house and put a stop to what's going on up there. It's sinful is what it is. We don't want that mess in our town." Said a voice I identified as Billie June Haltom. One of the ne'er do well Haltom family from out in the county. She wasn't a regular customer of Dixie's and I wondered how all these women had come to be gathered at the It'll Grow Back.

"No!" Ben shouted to the crowd, pulling my attention back. "Larry Gordon was not a vampire. He was a nice old man who didn't deserve what happened to him. And I intend to get to the bottom of it." His eyes scanned the crowd of women. "So be forewarned. I have some leads I'm following. If any of you knew. If the murderer is hiding in the crowd like the coward he, or *she*, is. I will find you."

The women got quiet. I saw Samantha Taylor, Doc Johnson's assistant at the morgue, elbow Sandra Goodwyn. Sandra shook her head and motioned to Ben.

He repeated that there was nothing illegal going on with the sleep study. That no one was looking for vampires. And that they should all go on home and let him worry about the testing. They didn't have to participate if they didn't want to. They could just boycott the whole thing.

That seemed to settle them down and they dispersed in groups of twos and threes, heads together and they continued to talk it over amongst themselves.

Dixie came up behind me and leaned out the door. "Thanks, Ben. I know this was hard on you."

"Did I hear a gun discharge when I drove up a few minutes ago?" He inquired.

"Must've been a truck backfiring somewhere."

"Since there doesn't seem to be anybody dead or wounded, I'm gonna let that slide this time." He gave her a sharp look. "I didn't know you kept a registered weapon on the premises."

Dixie shrank back into the shop. "You do now."

He got back into his car and drove off.

"Is that gun registered?"

"No. It's not. And Ben doesn't need to know that." She slid the gun into the drawer of her stylist station and glanced at my hair. "Let's get you

in the chair and get the ends trimmed
up. They're looking a bit bristly."

"I need to reschedule."

CHAPTER ELEVEN

The next morning I was contemplating the bristly ends of my still uncut hair in my bathroom mirror when I heard Elliott having cat hysterics outside. I'd let him out after he'd eaten his kibble and I headed upstairs to take a shower and get my day started.

What on earth had him raising Cain like this?

Hiking my robe up above my knees, I stepped up on the wooden stool I kept in the bathroom in order to see out of the small high set window facing the front yard. Craning my neck to get a look out and down, I caught a glimpse of bright blue, and red, and golden paint. And the curve of a wooden roof.

Holy Toledo! The fortune-teller was parked in my front yard. And, apparently, Elliott didn't like it at all. Didn't cats have some kind of sense of the paranormal? Was that what had him so stirred up?

I got down with a quickness, yanked on some jeans and a t-shirt and hustled downstairs.

Stopping to catch my breath before opening the front door, I remembered Dixie's words about big, scary guys hiding in the wagon. I thought about the pistol locked in the gun safe in the floor near the fireplace. It had belonged to my deceased husband and I'd never shot it.

Death said the Gypsy Queen

I glanced out the side window of the door and noticed Angela sitting at her table with the embroidered cloth. The crystal ball sat in the center with the morning sun painting a rainbow inside it as she sat calmly dealing some cards onto the table and totally ignoring Elliott. Who had is back arched as high as it would go and his fluffy coat of hair standing on end as he hissed and spat.

I decided to take my chances and leave the gun where it was.

As soon as I opened the door, Elliott ran straight at me and shot between my legs before I could move. Thank goodness I'd put on jeans. Otherwise the claws I felt scratching across the denim would be digging flesh as he went by.

Angela looked up and smiled. "What a beautiful morning." She said in greeting. As though it was the most normal thing in the world for her to be sitting here in my yard like this.

I stepped out onto the big front porch, pulling the door closed behind me.

"Come. Come." She said. "I won't bite you." And she smiled in a way that let me know that, somehow, she knew what was happening in this town.

I eased across the yard and up to the table, watchful in case someone else did actually jump out of the wagon. Nothing happened except Angela's amused expression. As though she were reading my mind. That thought sent a chill down my spine and I shivered. Goose walking over my grave, my mama used to say about that.

I sat tentatively in the chair across from Angela, leg muscles tense in case I needed to jump up and run, and watched in silence as she dealt the tarot cards in her hand. When she stopped laying cards on the table, she glanced at me.

"Do you want to know your future?"

"Nope." I replied. "The present is plenty for me."

She scooped up the cards, stacked them evenly together and wrapped them in a silk scarf, then laid them aside.

"You're wondering why I'm here. In your yard."

"I confess the thought crossed my mind."

Her laugh sounded like some lovely wind chimes I'd had years ago.

"I like you." She said. "I can see why Vlad is so fond of you."

I shifted in my chair. "Vlad?"

"Yes. My nephew." She replied. Like it was the most obvious thing in the world.

"But --" I thought back over everything I knew about Vlad. His parents had died in a car accident when

Vlad was ten. He'd moved away from Mercy, then. To live with his adoptive family. There hadn't been any family members to take him in. "Vlad doesn't have any blood kin." I said. "He was adopted by strangers after his parents died."

"It's true he was adopted by strangers." She conceded. "But only because I couldn't take in a young boy and raise him on my own."

"I've never heard him mention you." I said to her.

She raised an eyebrow. "Do you believe he tells you everything about his life?"

She had me there. Vlad and I had only recently begun to spend time together as something other than friends. It was so new and raw I certainly wasn't going to discuss it with this total stranger.

"Why aren't you parked up at the

Midnight Dragonfly instead of in my front yard?" I inquired.

"Vlad has enough troubles without me adding to them by parking my gypsy wagon in his yard."

She had a good point there. This wagon, and this woman, would only add to the turmoil already swirling after the secret testing revelation.

"So you decided to pick my home at random as your base while you're in town?"

"Not at random. I told you Vlad speaks highly of you." She paused. "There are two reasons I am here on your property. The first one being that if I parked my wagon at Vlad's home it would only lend credence to the words of those who are against him. Had I known his secret was already out, I would have come in disguise and left my wagon with friends until I could return to my home. The second reason I came to you is because I want you to help me to persuade him to give up this mad quest for answers to questions that are best left alone."

"I don't know what you're talking about." I told her.

She stared at me out of dark eyes. Searching my soul the way she'd done at the rest stop. I shifted in my chair, breaking the tension strung between us.

"You're loyal to him. I like that. But you *do* know what I'm talking about and I need your help."

"Why should I help you?"

She pointed a finger at the house behind me. "Look. There. By the steps going up."

I turned and followed her pointing finger. Squinting, I saw something small and white on the bottom step at the far edge. I hadn't noticed it as I was coming down the step since my attention had been focused on the intruder on my property. I walked over to investigate.

I stared down at the object sitting on the bottom step. A small doll wearing a white coat sat there staring back at me. It had fangs drawn on its cotton face. I turned and looked at Angela.

"Why did you put this doll here? Are you trying to scare me into helping you?"

She shook her head. "I didn't put it there. It was sitting there when I arrived early this morning. Someone must have sneaked here in the dark of night to leave it as a message for you."

I remembered thinking I'd heard something outside. But, that hadn't been last night. It was the night before. Could the doll have been here that long without me noticing? I didn't often use the front steps, so in was in the realm of possibility it'd been here that long. Another shiver chased its way down my spine. The thought of someone creeping around my home in the middle of the night unsettled me.

Cautiously, I reached down and picked it up. Lightening didn't strike me dead. Nothing fell out of the sky to kill me.

Taking that as a good sign, I examined the little doll more closely. It looked like something a child had made out of an old sock once I looked closely. The face drawn on with black ink. The white coat looked like it might have been taken from a doll's wardrobe. Who could have left it for me and what did they want me to do about it?

"It is a warning." Angela volunteered. Still sitting at her table.

"Of course you'd say it's a warning. That's how things operate in your world, right?" I shrugged, putting the doll back on the step for now. "Whatever it is, it's not scaring me away from anything."

I'd come a long way since the dead squirrel on my porch last year had sent me screaming for help to Ben and Dixie.

I glanced back at the doll. "Maybe someone's leaving me a clue instead of a warning. What do you think about that?"

"I wonder what *you* think about that. The message is for you."

I thought it over. Never in a month of Sundays would I have thought someone would be leaving me a vampire doll. But then, I'd never thought Vlad's secret testing would get out and freak out everyone in town. Which just goes to show how naïve a person can be.

"Maybe it's Doc Johnson. He wears a white lab coat. Maybe there's something he's not seeing in the case with Larry Gordon." I glanced at her. "That's the man who was murdered with a stake through his heart. How did you know about that, anyway?"

"I didn't." Angela answered. She shifted in her chair. "It was a total coincidence that I met you and your friend at that rest stop. I recognized you as soon as you got out of your car. And decided to play a little game on you." She smiled mischievously. "That's the truth. As much as I hate to admit to you that it wasn't something I arranged through paranormal powers."

"So your sole purpose in coming to Mercy was to warn Vlad to stop the DNA testing for the vampire gene?"

She nodded.

"And, now it's too late to do that. The cat's out of the bag."

She nodded again, looking rueful. "Yes. I wish I'd come much sooner."

Death said the Gypsy Queen

I looked at the colorful wagon. "How did you get to the rest stop? And here? Is there an invisible truck sitting in my yard somewhere?"

Angela laughed that wonderful laugh again. "No. I have a friend who moves it with his truck. He's gone right now. But he'll be back when I need him."

"Do you call him on the phone when you want to move the wagon?"

"Of course." She said. "What did you think? Mental telepathy?"

"You're kind of a smart ass." I said.

"You should know. You're one yourself."

I stood up. "I'll think about what you've said. And what you've asked me to do. No promises."

She gave me a smile. "It's all I can ask."

"I'm going in now. To get dressed and then I'll be heading out to meet with some people."

"Of course. I will be right here awaiting you're answer."

Why did that sound like a threat? I wondered. I made my way into the house and dodged a still angry Elliott who met me with snarls and claws when I started up the stairs. Angela had rocked his kitty world. Should I take that as a warning that I shouldn't take anything she told me at face value?

CHAPTER TWELVE

I pulled out of my driveway in the mustang an hour later with the weird little doll riding shotgun.

Angela had been inside her wagon -- or somewhere out of my line of sight -- when I came back out of the house. Which was a relief. I hadn't wanted to feel obligated to make conversation with her again so soon.

While I was showering and getting dressed, I decided to take the doll to Doc Johnson and get his opinion. If the doll was meant to resemble him, maybe it would jog something in his mind that the doll was supposed to represent.

I didn't look forward to tangling with Jimmy John, so I was relieved when I called Doc and he told me to meet him in the cafeteria. He'd just sat down to a sandwich and coffee.

Doc took the little doll in his hands and examined it. Turning it repeatedly. Touching the white jacket. Rubbing his fingers over the inked in face.

"What do you think?" I asked. "Kinda spooky, right?"

Doc laid the doll down on the table between us and sipped his coffee. "I don't know that I think it's particularly spooky. It's homemade. There aren't any manufacturer tags on it."

At my look, he went on. "Just because something is crudely made, doesn't mean it's homemade. I've paid high dollar for some things that fell apart right off the bat."

I picked up the doll and turned it in my own hands, taking in the crudeness of it. And the lack of a label. "What do you think it means?"

He shrugged. "Could be any number of things. I assume those are vampire fangs drawn in the mouth area. Maybe it's some kind of reference to Larry Gordon."

I hadn't considered it from that angle and spent a few minutes rolling it over in my mind. But that dog didn't hunt for me.

"I don't think that's it." I gave him a sideways glance. "I actually thought it might be supposed to represent you."

He choked a bit on the coffee he's just sipped.

"You think I'm secretly a vampire?"

"Of course not." I protested. "I thought maybe someone was insinuatin' that you overlooked something in the Larry Gordon autopsy."

"Hm. Seems like you're reaching to me."

He picked up the doll again. "Besides. This doll has long hair and I'm bald as an egg. Maybe it's Don over at the barbershop. He wears those white jackets when he's cutting hair."

I gave it some thought. "But Don's hair isn't long like this. So, if it's not you because you're bald, then by the same deduction it can't be Don because the hair on the doll is long and Don's is short."

"Maybe someone at the animal clinic? Mary Goodwyn or her daughter Sandra? Don't they wear white coats?" He rubbed his chin thoughtfully. "Or, how about my morgue assistant, Samantha Taylor. She was one of the first participants in the sleep study." He paused. "Or maybe her ne'er-do-well -- and not terribly bright - brothers are involved.

The way he emphasized the words *sleep study* made me realize he knew about the secret testing, too. "Did she tell you her results? The Taylors are one of the oldest families in the county."

"She did not." He held up a hand. "And I didn't ask. It's none of my business."

"I would think it would be important for you to know things like that about someone working with you in this job."

"Nothing in the hiring policies about genetic anomalies. But, I admit I'm curious." He leaned closer and whispered to me. "I snuck up there and did a quick overnight testing. And I do not have the genetic anomaly Vlad's looking for. As a doctor, I'm not sure if I'm disappointed. But as a citizen of Mercy, and seeing that stake through old Larry's heart, I'm glad I don't."

I slapped my hands down on the table, drawing attention from people nearby. I smiled and waved, waiting til they went back to their own business.

Keeping my voice low, I said, "Do you think someone has gotten access to Vlad's records and is conducting some kind of personal vendetta?"

"I have no idea. That's a question for Vlad to answer."

I sat back in my chair defeated.

"Don't give up." Doc said as he got up from his chair, crumpling the wrapping from his sandwich in his hand. "I'm sure there's some meaning or warning behind the doll and we just haven't figured it out. Are you going to take it to Ben and see what he thinks?"

I got up and pushed the chair in to the table. "That's where I'm headed next." I tucked the doll into my purse and followed Doc out of the cafeteria.

I found Ben in his office, filling out paperwork. Reenie, his dispatcher, wasn't at her desk when I came in so I'd come straight to his door. He looked up when he realized someone was standing in his there and motioned me to the chair in front of his desk. Pushing the paperwork aside, he asked, "What can I do for you, Cuz?"

I took the doll from my purse and laid it on his desk. He picked it up and looked a question at me.

"That was sittin' on my front steps this morning."

He quirked an eyebrow. "No note? Just this doll?"

"Yep. Just the doll."

Ben turned it in his hands just like Doc had done. "Too bad it's not made of something that would hold fingerprints instead of this cloth. Although fingerprints would be ruined by now with you handling it."

I stiffened with insult. "I know better than to handle something that you could get fingerprints off of."

"Simmer down." He told me. "No need to get your feathers ruffled."

I sat back. Letting my temper ease up. Frustration with the meaning of the doll had gotten me more upset than the situation warranted.

"I went by the hospital first to see if Doc had any thoughts on it."

"And did he?"

"No." I sighed. "I told him I thought maybe someone meant it to be him and that maybe he'd missed something in the autopsy of Larry Gordon."

Ben tossed the doll back to me "I bet he didn't think too much of that theory."

I put the doll back in my purse. "No. He didn't."

Ben leaned back in his chair making the leather creak. "I'm more concerned that someone came on your property and left this for you." He drummed his fingers on the desk. "You didn't hear anything?"

I shook my head. "And that reminds me." I changed the subject before he could decide he needed to move in with me. Or me with him until the case was solved. "That fortune-teller is parked in my front yard."

Ben sat up straight. "You're kidding me. How did that come to be?"

I gave him the explanation she'd given me and he didn't like it.

"Are you going deaf in your old age? I can understand how you wouldn't hear someone sneaking around leaving the doll. But you seriously didn't hear a truck pull in with a wagon?"

"My bedroom is on the back of the house. And I don't know what kind of truck it was. Maybe it was a quiet one. Not everyone wants their truck to be loud."

He took a bottle of antacid from his desk drawer and popped two.

"It must not have been a diesel then. Surely to goodness you'd've heard *that.*"

"Is there any new information on the case?" I asked, changing the subject. "Did y'all find anything at the scene that might point to a suspect?"

He popped another antacid. "Not a dang thing."

I propped my elbow on the chair arm and leaned my chin on my hand. "I'm trying to picture how someone could've killed him without anyone seeing or realizing it sooner."

"He was stabbed before the farmer's market opened. And it took that long for someone to head over to the restrooms and find him."

I thought about it. The farmer's market opened at nine. And Dixie and I had arrived just after noon. We hadn't been there more than fifteen or twenty minutes when Darla started screaming. But, that was a big window of time during which no one needed to relieve himself or herself. I pictured the cinderblock building and the way the exterior ells had been built to offer privacy. It kept the body hidden from any casual glances in that direction. Maybe.

"So what was the time of death? I forgot to ask Doc when I was over there."

"Eight AM give or take a bit."

"I wonder what Larry was doing out there that early. Did he have a booth?"

"Nope."

He looked glum at the lack of evidence. He'd yet to come up with a single suspect. And neither had I. A tricky killer indeed.

"What about all those women that were making threats over at the It'll Grow Back the other day. Have any of them pulled anything else?"

Ben shook his head. "It's been quiet on that front. Thank goodness. I wish we had some idea of who printed up and distributed those fliers. It has to be someone connected with the crime."

I realized I hadn't gotten a flyer at my house. "Did you get a flyer at your house?" I asked Ben. He shook his head. "Neither did I. That's interesting. Were you able to get any fingerprints off the flyers the ladies had."

Ben rolled his eyes. "Lots of prints. And nothing we can use. There were prints from everyone and their sister on them."

Ouch.

"So where does that leave us? Not even one suspect?"

"Not. One."

I filled him in on Doc's theory about the testing and that the killer was someone who had somehow gotten access to the secret testing results.

"I talked to Vlad about it."

Ben sat up in his chair, giving me a hard look. "When did you talk to Vlad?"

I gulped. "Hasn't he called you back?"

Ben shook his head. "No. He hasn't."

"Well, I thought he was going to." I defended myself. "I was going to leave him a voice message about the person who called my house and gave me a creepy warning about the secret testing."

"What! What creepy message?"

Oops! I'd forgotten to tell Ben about the call. The mob scene at Dixie's shop had driven it from my head.

"I'm sorry." I apologized to Ben. "It was the night before the big ruckus at Dixie's. I clean forgot about it."

He settled back in his chair. "Someone definitely has it in for Vlad. I wonder why they called *you*?"

I shrugged. "It's pretty common knowledge around town that I was one of his friends back in the day." I shifted in my chair. "And possibly that he and I are spending time together these days."

Ben grinned. "You're blushing." Then he shifted back into cop mode. "It has to be someone you know since they had your phone number. Give me your phone and I'll do a reverse number look up."

I shook my head. "Whoever it was called on my landline. And that number is in the phone book. It could be anyone. I think it's a woman, though. Something about the timber of the voice – even though she was disguising it."

Ben grimaced. "I forgot you have that landline. Clever of the caller to use that number. Much harder to trace. I can get with the phone company and request all incoming calls to your house, but that'll take time." He sighed.

CHAPTER THIRTEEN

As I drove past Miss Edna's on my way home, Harley Ann rushed down the front walk and waved me to the curb. I groaned inwardly. I wasn't prepared to discuss the case – or lack thereof – with Miss Edna just yet. However, I couldn't find it in my heart to pretend I didn't see the redheaded girl standing there waving clear as day.

I pulled over and rolled down the window. "How're you today?"

"I'm so glad I caught you, Lily Gayle. Aunt Edna and I were just speculating on the case this morning and wondering why we haven't heard from you." Harley Ann's eyes rolled toward the porch and I noticed Miss Edna sitting in her favorite chair with her 'bird watching' binoculars around her neck.

"Aunt Edna was just saying as how she was going to call you in a little while and here you are like it was meant to be."

I quirked an eyebrow. Harley Ann leaned a bit closer and whispered. "She's mad as a hornet and loaded for bear. It might be best to go ahead and deal with her now."

I sighed and put the car in park.

As I followed Harley Ann up onto the porch, I felt the scorch of Miss Edna's displeasure sear across me.

"Well, well, well. Look who has graced us with her presence."

Not a good start.

"Hey there, Miss Edna. I've been meaning to give you a call or come by for a visit. But you know how time gets away from you." I sat in the chair across from her. Closest to the steps in case I needed to make a quick exit.

"How about a glass of tea and some biscuits with my vanilla honey butter?" Harley Ann asked, picking up the cut glass pitcher off the table and pouring tea into an extra glass. She set it in front of me and passed the linen wrapped biscuits in the silver basket. They sure were doing it up fancy today. I pulled a biscuit from the cloth and began slathering it with the butter as though Miss Edna wasn't about ready to spit nails.

"I'm about to start on a new dress for a customer." I said into the heavy silence.

"Is that right?" Harley Ann responded. "What kind of dress?"

"Would you believe this customer insists she's related to Queen Victoria? She wants a ball gown that's an exact replica of one worn by Victoria in 1872. And emailed me a picture of it to boot."

"There no accounting for some people's doin's." Miss Edna remarked. "Like the ones who are supposed to be keeping a person informed about a case they're working on together."

I shrugged. "There's not been anything to tell, Miss Edna."

"Well how about you tell me what's going on with the rainbow colored wagon parked in your front yard for starters?" Miss Edna said sharply.

At my startled glance, she went on. "I'm old. Not senile. And I have people who pass information on to me.

Even if you don't."

Good Lord. She sounded like a cranky two-year old.

"As a matter of fact the woman in the wagon is Vlad's aunt, Angela. She's come to try and talk Vlad out of his secret testing. But it seems it's not quite so secret anymore."

"A woman of wisdom." Miss Edna remarked. "Too bad she didn't get here sooner."

"I have no idea how the information got out all over town." I said. "I mean before those flyers were left at every house in town. And maybe in the county, too."

"Information is power." Miss Edna said. "You know that as well as I do. We just choose not to use it for harm."

I giggled, earning a sharp look from Miss Edna and a smile from Harley Ann.

"You make us sound like some kind

of comic book super heroes." I said. "Maybe I should make capes for all of us."

Miss Edna sniffed. "Be that as it may, I'm glad you finally found a minute to stop by here. I was telling Harley Ann earlier that I should get in touch with you and pass along some new information."

I was all ears, leaning forward.

"Is it a suspect we can check out? Ben's pretty unhappy about not having someone to question yet."

Miss Edna folded her napkin and put it across her plate. "Unfortunately, no. I've been hearing some more rumors about people being very angry about Vlad sneaking around like he's been doing. Testing people without their knowledge. Folks are wondering if this state funded testing was a trick all along to get personal genetic information about people for some kind of undercover government project." She frowned. "They're calling it 'dark blood' and are pretty unhappy that people with it have been living among us for years without anyone knowing."

I sat back, dumbfounded. "That's crazy."

"Maybe." Miss Edna said. "But folks are scared of things they don't understand. You know that."

"Yes. But this seems over the top. It's not like anyone with the gene is suddenly going to start going around biting people and drinking their blood. These people have been our friends and neighbors for years."

I remembered the marks on Larry Gordon's neck and Doc's speculation that they were human bite marks and suddenly wondered if maybe people *were* going around biting necks and drinking blood. A recluse like Larry Gordon would be a perfect target.

I filled Miss Edna and Harley Ann in on the autopsy findings and Doc's speculations.

"There. You see?" Miss Edna stated. "It's already started."

"You said that it's most likely the oldest families in the county that have the gene, because they were all circus performers originally and using the circus to hide their differences, right?" Asked Harley Ann.

I nodded.

"I have something that may or may not be suspicious. It didn't strike me that way at the time, but in hindsight it could be." She fiddled with her napkin and I waited patiently. "I hate to throw suspicion on someone who maybe didn't do anything wrong. Because of spending time in prison for helping my boyfriend and having no idea he was robbing that place I'm pretty sensitive about people getting accused of things."

"Land sakes, girl! Spit it out!" Miss Edna said in an exasperated voice.

"Friday afternoon I was out at the farmer's market field looking at the tables there and deciding which one I wanted to try and get Saturday. Since it was my first time there I wanted to do really well."

She shifted in her chair, clearly torn about the information she was about to share.

"I saw Sandra Goodwyn and Samantha Taylor out by the restroom building. And Mrs. Goodwyn was sitting in her car by herself. I didn't really think much about it at the time. I just assumed they stopped there to use the facilities." She looked into our eyes. "And maybe that's exactly what they *were* doing. But I thought I should tell you anyway."

"The Taylors and the Goodwyns are both founding families. And, more than likely related to each other if you trace them far enough back. *And* good candidate to be carrying the gene." Miss Edna said.

"A lot of the families here are distant cousins. They've lived here for so many generations and married into each other." I added.

"Do you think Vlad has found out that they carry the gene for the vampire blood?" Harley Ann asked.

"It's pretty likely that he has." Snapped Miss Edna. "That's why he came here isn't it. To find the others here who have it. And look what a mess he's made of our town with his curiosity."

"The others?" Harley Ann asked.

"Well, of course, Vlad has it. Why else would he be looking for that gene if he didn't?" Miss Edna snapped at her niece.

Harley Ann looked at me, big-eyed. I guess she'd figured out Vlad and I were beginning to have romantic feelings.

"It sounds to me like the next step is for you to go up to the Midnight Dragonfly, Lily Gayle, and exert your charms on the good doctor to find out what he's found out." Miss Edna said.

I silently agreed. We needed to know what he'd found out. And I needed to get on to him about his aunt being parked in my yard. I now felt like he hadn't been in a dead zone when we'd talked. He'd heard what I said and didn't want to tell me it was his aunt out there.

More importantly, I wanted to discuss holding off on the testing for a bit. The sleep apnea one, too. At this point people wouldn't trust him about what he was doing with their blood. I placed a bet with myself that he'd had no more people signing up for the study now that word had gotten out about what he was up to.

There was murder happening and no one wanted to get in line for that.

CHAPTER FOURTEEN

I pulled to a stop at the foot of the steps leading up the the elegant front door of the old Mitchell Manor that had been transformed in to the Midnight Dragonfly a little over a year ago. Then shut down as a B&B and reopened as a sleep study clinic by Vlad not quite a year ago. Lots of changes in this sleepy little town.

The minute I entered the lobby area, I was met by a steely-eyed man in scrubs asking my business here.

"I'm here to speak to Doctor Templeton. Tell him it's Lily Gayle Lambert."

"Is he expecting you?" Inquired steely-eyes.

"No." I said. "But I'm sure he'll find time for me if you'll just go tell him I'm here."

The man gave me a rude once-over. "Wait here."

I stood around admiring the refinished wood floors and tasteful artwork for nearly fifteen minutes before Vlad finally showed up. Inwardly I fumed about steely-eyes. What a jerk. When I heard Vlad's voice behind me, I jumped a little. I hadn't heard him come in.

"Lily Gayle. What bring you up here?"

I turned and gave him a once over. Not a hair out of place. And no indication that the town was going nuts over his sneaky project.

"There's something I need to talk to you about that can't wait." I gave a significant look at steely-eyes who'd followed Vlad into the lobby area. "Alone."

Vlad turned and said. "We're fine here, Dan."

With a final suspicious look, Dan left us alone. Vlad took me by the hand and led me to one of the former parlors. It didn't look much different from when the place had its opening night party as a bed and breakfast and I remarked on it.

"Yes. We felt that it could serve as a meeting room without changing anything." Vlad motioned me to one of the wingback chairs. "What's this all about?"

"A couple of things, actually." I settled back more comfortably in the chair. This could take some time. "Your aunt, Angela and her wagon are parked in my front yard."

"*What?*"

"That's right. She came here looking for me because she wants me to help her persuade you to stop your genetic testing."

"When did she get here?"

"Dixie and I met her at the rest stop outside of town on Highway 7 on our way back from Oxford Saturday. She tried to scare the crap out of me with dire warnings of vampire blood." I gave him a sharp look. "Like I told you on the phone."

He grimaced. "That sounds like something she'd do. She loves all that gypsy fortune-teller stuff she does for a living."

"She also didn't bother to tell me who she really was until she was parked in my yard." I added.

"She has a mind of her own. Which

I guess you figured out already. Thank you for letting me know. I'll have a talk with her about how she's acting." He picked a stray string off his slacks. "You said there were two things. What's the second one?"

Seriously? That was it on Aunt Angela? I decided to let it go for the moment. Her being in my yard didn't really matter at this point anyway.

"Are you aware of the flyer that pretty much everyone in town received that outed your little secret testing project?" I asked.

Vlad sighed as he ran his hand through his dark hair. "Yes. Ben called to let me know what happened so we'd be watching out for anything strange going on up here. And to increase our security."

"I hate to say I told you so….but I told you so."

He leaned back in his chair,

resting his head against the high back, and I noticed the dark circles under his eyes. He must not have been getting much rest lately. "Yes. You did tell me so. But this project is so important. I *had* to do it, Lily Gayle. It can be the start of some real medical help for people with the genetic anomaly. Children could be able to live normal lives instead of always being shut into their homes. Medicine has made some strides. I'm a good example. But my anomaly is weaker than some. There are those out there that can't get any benefit from currently available treatments."

His passion had blinded him to the consequences of the way he'd chosen to obtain his research.

"Why didn't you present it to everyone in town just the way you said it now? Why the sneaking around?"

He clinched his fingers on the arms of the chair. "You see what happened when they found out. It's ridiculous, in this day and age, for grown people to be acting like this. And yet they are. They'd never have gone along with it if I'd told them about it up front."

"What about Larry Gordon? Did he have the gene?"

"Yes. But I don't see how that contributed to his murder."

"Don't be naïve, Vlad. He's dead *because* of it. Because someone in this town found out and is so scared of that gene that they killed him. I'm worried more will die before the killer is found. How is the information getting out?"

He stood and paced the small room. "I don't know. I've always been very security conscious. Right from the first day. All of the information is logged into the computer and only myself and two other people have access to the computer. And I'm the only one with access to the genetic anomaly testing information."

"Who are the other two people with access to the computer? Are they local?"

He stopped pacing. "Yes. But I trust them implicitly. They were highly recommended."

"Who are they and who recommended them?"

"Sandra Goodwyn and Samantha Taylor. Sandra is a vet tech here in town working at her mama's clinic and Samantha works in the morgue with Doctor Johnson. Both had recommendations from their employer."

"I know both of them." I told him. "What, exactly, do they do for you here? I didn't even know they were working here."

"It's just a few hours a week in the evening. They key in information from the sleep apnea study. That's all. They have no access to the other study. I don't think they even knew I was conducting it until those flyers came out."

I sighed. "I wouldn't be too sure about that. As far as I know, both girls are good, upstanding citizens. But people get curious. Or they get bored. And they start pilfering around and looking at things that are none of their business. And, not to paint anyone with the brush of suspicion, but Samantha's brothers are not above some shady activity if it will get them easy money."

He flung himself back into the chair across from me, clearly frustrated. "I can't believe this is happening."

"You'll have a talk with Ben and he can pull them in for questioning about it."

But before that happened, I intended to do a little investigating on my own.

CHAPTER FIFTEEN

I pulled into the parking lot of the FurBabies animal clinic on the outskirts of town without a game plan. But I've always been quick on my feet so I'd decided to wing it. Hopefully things wouldn't blow up in my face.

There were only two cars in the lot and I hoped both belong to the Goodwyns. I didn't think Mary would talk to me with customers in house. And she shouldn't. This was her business. But, being the impatient kind of gal I am, I didn't want to wait till this evening when she was at home to ask my questions. And I didn't want to delay Ben too much in setting up a meeting to question Sandra about her activities at the sleep study.

A bell chimed when I entered. The waiting area was empty, but almost immediately Mary Goodwyn came out of the exam room across the hall. She pulled up short when she saw me. Empty handed.

"Why, hello, Lily Gayle. Is Elliott okay?"

"Yes. He's fine. At home sleeping off his morning kibble." I glanced around, but didn't see anyone else here. Who did the second car belong to? Maybe Sandra was in the back somewhere. Definitely no one waiting here, and no one had come out of the exam room with Mary.

Mary's brows drew together. "Have you cut back on Elliott's food like I recommended? He's too fat."

I tried to hide a guilty flush rising in my face. I hadn't cut back on his kibble. Yet. I'd tried that a couple of years ago and he'd made my life miserable until I upped his servings again.

"Actually, I'm here to double check some genealogy information on your family." Okay. Thinking on my feet would commence now.

She raised an eyebrow. "You're doing genealogy research on my family? Why?"

"Not just *your* family." I hastened to assure her, making up my story as I went along. "I'm doing a book on the founding families of Mercy. And the Goodwyn are one of them."

"Yes. That's true." She motioned me to the chairs in the waiting area.

Death said the Gypsy Queen

"Let's sit while we talk."

I glanced at the wooden benches that served as seating in the waiting area. Uncomfortable as all get out. But practical for her business in case pets decided to throw up – or other messy business – while waiting to see the doctor. She'd softened the harsh look with plants.

"Wow. Poinsettias in September! You must really have a green thumb." I remarked as I noticed a row of them on top of the shelves displaying flea and tick powder for pets.

Mary made a shushing sound, finger to her lips. "Don't let Miss Edna hear you say that. She'll run you out of town for treasonous thoughts."

I laughed. "It's good for her to have some competition. Even though she'd never admit that anyone is as good with plants as she is."

Mary motioned me to a chair. "I

brought in some cookies from home. Let me get us some to munch on while we're chatting. It's a new recipe and I'd like to get your opinion on them."

She bustled off somewhere in the back as I sat looking around the room. This was the first time I'd ever been here when no one was waiting with a cranky pet in need of medical attention. Aside from the benches, products on shelving and plants, there wasn't much to see. Some outdated magazines lay scattered along the bench and that covered it. To pass the time, I did some mental gymnastics as I worked out my cover story.

Mary came back with a two small paper plates of cookies and two bottles of water. I took the plate she held out to me inhaling the delicious scent of the cookies. I took a big bite of one and my mouth flooded with sweet cinnamon flavor and something I couldn't quite identify.

"Wow, Mary! This is absolutely delicious. I can taste cinnamon, but what else is in it? I looked closely at my cookie. "And what are these neat little red and green sprinkles on top?" I picked some off the cookie and rolled them in my fingertips. "I don't think I've ever seen anything like them before." I laughed. "Of course, cooking and baking are not my forte, so anybody else might know what they are at a glance."

Mary smiled. "You're right about the cinnamon. But the rest is a secret. Can't have Harley Ann taking all the credit for the best sweets in town, can we?"

She settled back more comfortably in her chair. "So. The Goodwyns. What is it you're looking for in the way of information?"

"Oh I'm not sure. Maybe old

letters? Or Bible's with birth, wedding and death date entries? Or journals would be good."

"Ha! The Goodwyns are not the journal keeping kind. They don't spend much time writing down their thoughts. Goodwyns are *much* better at acting on their thoughts."

"Well, anything you can find that might flesh out the basic census record information would be really helpful." I finished the first cookie and started on the second one. They really were good.

"I've decided to sign up for the sleep study Vlad Templeton is doing." She said out of the blue.

I choked down the last of the cookie. She'd taken me by surprise with that statement.

"Why are you going to do that? I saw you at the confab at Dixie's the other day so I know you know that Vlad is doing something other than sleep apnea testing."

If I'd thought I was going to catch her off guard I'd been mistaken.

"That's exactly why I want to do the testing. As a doctor myself I'm fascinated by the thought of genetic anomalies running through the citizens of Mercy. Even if a lot of others aren't so happy about the idea. You should keep your eyes open wide til the murder is solved. You never know who might be hiding something."

Well color me amazed. I'd never have pegged her for someone in favor of the testing. And was she trying to warn me about someone in particular. Or just everyone in general.

"You aren't scared that someone might come after you because of the testing? I'm wondering if Vlad should just stop them until this murder is solved."

Mary looked thoughtful, but at that moment, the front door opened and Sandra Goodwyn came in. She stopped when she saw the two of us chatting in the waiting area. And Mary didn't answer my question.

"Hey, Lily Gayle. This is a surprise." She sat in the chair next to her mama and snagged a cookie off her plate. "I got those supplies unboxed and put away in the storage unit out back, Mama. What are the two of you up to?" She asked, munching a cookie.

"Lily Gayle came by to ask about information on the Goodwyns for a book she's writing on the founding families of Mercy."

Sandra eyed me over her cookie. "Like the Mitchells?"

"Well, all of the Mitchells are dead and buried. Or in jail. So the segment on them will be a bit short. I'll put in some of the information

187

that I found when I was doing the genealogy search for LizBeth a couple of years ago. They were the original settlers and the ones who named the town. That's pretty pertinent to a history of the town."

Sandra drank some of her mama's water, then said. "Yeah. The Mitchells turned out to be some kind of surprise, didn't they? Who knew a werewolf was living right here in Mercy all those years?"

I didn't much like the avid look in her eyes. "He wasn't a werewolf." I said. "He was just a poor guy with a genetic anomaly that made him grow extra hair. It's a pity the Mitchells were so medieval about the whole situation. Things could have been so different."

Sandra finished off another cookie and said. "There are still Mitchell relations in town. I'm surprised you didn't uncover that with all of your research you did."

"Sandra!" Mary exclaimed. "Don't be rude."

"None so blind as those who will not see." Sandra said.

"Don't quote the Bible to your own crude uses." Mary said. "And I already asked you to stop being rude."

"I'm not being rude. I'm just saying I'm surprised is all." She turned her eyes to me. "Samantha Taylor told me they're kin to the Mitchells way back. On the wrong side of the blanket if you get my drift."

I did get her drift. And, frankly, it wouldn't surprise me in the least. The Mitchells had always figured they were the lords of all they surveyed around here. So why not the womenfolk?

"You hush up with that talk, Sandra Dee Goodwyn. Right this minute."

Death said the Gypsy Queen

I masked a laugh at the girl's middle name with a cough. Guess Mary had been a fan of the original Sandra Dee. Or maybe Olivia Newton John in Grease.

"I was talking with Vlad earlier today and he told me you and Samantha are working part time doing data entry for him on his sleep apnea study." I said to break the tension between mother and daughter.

Sandra's eyes narrowed. Then the look disappeared and I wondered if I'd imagined it.

"Yes. Sam and I are both in need of some extra income. I'm saving up for a new car. I don't know what it is she's saving for. She's being pretty secretive about it, whatever it is."

I knew Samantha Taylor wanted to go to college and figured she was saving for that. I had no idea why she would keep the information secret from her friend though. I shrugged mentally.

"So," I said to Sandra. "You two only handle the sleep apnea information? Nothing else?"

Sandra yawned. "If you mean information about that *other* DNA testing he's doing, then no, we don't have any access to it."

Her rude attitude grated on my nerves. However, the comment about the genetic testing perked me right up.

"When did you realize he was doing some additional tests?" I asked. Careful to keep my voice casual.

She gave me a level stare. As though she knew I was fishing for information that might be useful in Ben's investigation. Or my own for that matter.

"Yesterday. Like everybody else in town." She emphasized. "We got one of those flyers on our door, too." She turned to her mother. "Didn't we, mama?"

Mary Goodwyn hesitated just the slightest bit, making me wonder if there was something she wasn't saying. I figured a mama would protect her child if said child had done something bad, but not illegal.

But Mary glanced over at me and said. "Yes. We did get one of those flyers. What are you implying, Lily Gayle? Have you asked Samantha Taylor these same questions? Or do you plan to?"

Uh. Oh. I could see I'd get no more information here, so I rose. "Not a thing, Mary. Just making some inquiries. I'll see y'all later."

As I exited the building, I made a mental note to run out to the Taylor's place tomorrow and have a chat with Samantha.

Preferably when her brothers

weren't around. I'd had a misunderstanding with them a couple of years ago when I was working on the wolf man case and went into their trailer without their permission. They'd been pretty riled up about it. Especially since I'd found some evidence there that tied them in with the crime.

Don't borrow trouble, my mama used to tell me. And I wouldn't. But, I couldn't face talking with one more person today. I was peopled out.

CHAPTER SIXTEEN

When I opened my eyes I thought it was still night. I couldn't see a blame thing. I felt Elliott marching back and forth across my belly the way he does when his breakfast is late, but it couldn't be late because it was still dark. I pushed him off me and got a nip to my fingers from his sharp teeth to protest the treatment.

Sliding to the side of the bed, I switched on the lamp on the table there. Nothing. My heart started pounding like a bass drum.

I scrambled my fingers across the bedside table searching for my phone. When my fingers touched it, I grabbed it and held it up in front of me. Nothing. No light at all. I should be able to see the phone screen even in the dark.

What the hell?

Elliott nudged my hand, looking for some petting. My first instinct was to push him away again so I could think without distractions. But his fur was soft and reassuring under my fingers and his purr made me feel less scared.

Okay. Think, girl. I couldn't see. Fact. I had no idea why. Fact. I hadn't suffered a blow to the head or a fall that might contribute to a delayed impact on my vision. Fact. This was going nowhere fast. Fact.

I needed reinforcements.

"Hey, Siri." When I heard the tone indicating Siri was listening, I said. "Call Dixie."

"Did you mean call Dick's son?" asked Siri.

I took a couple of deep breaths trying to calm myself to the point that my pronunciation would be understandable.

"Hey, Siri." I tried again. At the tone indicating she was listening, I said. "Call Dixie."

"Calling Dixie." Siri said. Much to my relief.

As soon as she answered, I talked right over her. "Dixie! I'm blind. I don't know what happened but I can't see a dern thing. Please come over here and run me to the emergency room."

"I'm on my way."

That was Dixie for you. No tiresome questions and explanations. Just that she was on her way. Cool as a cucumber in a crises. I felt around the foot of the bed for the clothes I'd taken off last night. I didn't want to go to the hospital in my nightgown.

It seemed to take Dixie forever to get to my house. But maybe that was because I couldn't do anything but sit here and wait. I was scared to try and go downstairs in case I tripped and fell adding broken bones to the problem.

Dixie had a key and I knew she'd use it to get in. Once she actually got here. Which I hoped was soon. My knee started jumping in agitation. I put my hand on it to hold it in place.

Elliott jumped off the bed with a soft thump of kitty feet. I heard his toenails clicking on the wood flooring in the hallway, then the sound of a key turning in the lock downstairs.

Thank goodness

"Dixie?" I hollered. "I'm up

here."

"I figured you would be." She said from the direction of the bedroom door. She gotten up the stairs in double time.

I held out my hand and she took it. I hadn't realize mine was freezing until her warm one enclosed it.

She pulled me to my feet and guided me across the room. "Come on. We'll get you to the ER and they'll figure this out in no time."

I stumbled along, not completely trusting her, or myself. Making sure I had both feet firmly planted on each step before moving to the next one. Dixie held my arm tight and kept her mouth shut, letting me concentrate. At last we made it outside to her car.

"Is the gypsy wagon still out here?"

"Gypsy wagon? Are you talking about the fortune-teller we met out on the highway?"

"Yes. Didn't I tell you she showed up in my yard a couple of days ago?"

Dixie pushed me gently into the passenger seat of her car. "There's no wagon here now. And. No. You didn't. Why was she here at your house? Was she trying to get money from you?"

I waited until Dixie had gone around the the driver's side, gotten in and cranked the car.

"She's Vlad's aunt."

Stunned silence greet that statement.

"You are kidding me." She finally said.

"Nope. She was on her way here to try and persuade Vlad to stop the vampire gene testing and we just happened to run into her at that rest stop. She admitted to me it was a complete coincidence."

Dixie started driving into town.

"Well. I'm glad she was honest with you. I told you there's no such thing as being able to foresee the future. If she could do that she'd've known to get her butt here a month or more ago to stop Vlad."

"I wonder where she got to?"

Dixie snorted. "Who cares? It's better she's not around with that wagon and those clothes. Everyone is already on edge all over town. Her running around as Vlad's fortune-teller aunt might just tip the scales out of balance. In a bad way."

I heard the blinker turn on and click. Dixie braked to a stop and said. "We're here. Sit tight while I run in and get somebody with a wheel chair. That way you won't have to try to walk."

It wasn't long before the car door opened and a hand grasped my arm just above the elbow.

"Hey, Lily Gayle. What have you

gotten yourself into now." Asked a female voice that seemed familiar but I couldn't quite place it.

"Who's that?" I inquired.

"Oh. Sorry. I wasn't thinking. It's me. Samantha Taylor. I'm picking up some extra work helping out in the ER when Doc Johnson doesn't need me."

I stood and let her guide me into a wheelchair.

"You sure are a busy young lady." I commented. "Vlad told me you're helping out up there, too."

Her hands tightened to a pinch on my arms and I yelped.

"Oh! I'm so sorry, Lily Gayle. I didn't mean to pinch your arms like that."

"I got her paperwork filled in, Samantha." Said Dixie, sounding out of breath. "We can take her on into one of the rooms to wait for a doctor."

Samantha's hands released my

arms. I felt the chair begin to move and heard the electronic doors whoosh open. Cold air flowed out and over me.

I was rolled in a couple of different directions, then to a halt. "Here we are." Samantha said.

"I'll take it from here." Dixie told her. "You must have other things more important to be doing."

Samantha laughed and patted my arm gently where she'd pinched it earlier. Was that some kind of message? I couldn't decide and didn't want to ask while I wasn't in any position to run.

"Everything's important in here. Y'all just holler if you need anything while you're waiting."

I heard rubber soled shoes squeak out of the room.

CHAPTER SEVENTEEN

Two hours, and a whole lot of frustration later, I sat tucked up into a hospital bed. No one could figure out what was wrong with me, so I was being kept for observation.

"You go on home, Dixie. There's no point in you staying here with me. I'll be fine."

"I wouldn't feel right leaving you here by yourself when you can't see a blessed thing. What if somebody decides to get you out of the way of investigating the murder? You'd never know they were in here."

"Way to make me feel safe, Dix."
I shivered and wasn't sure if it was
the air conditioning or the thought of
someone being in the room with me that
I couldn't see.

Her hand covered mine. "I'm
sorry. I didn't mean to scare you."

"Well, what did you *think* would
happen with that kind of talk?" I heard
Miss Edna say and wasn't sure if I was
glad she'd come or not.

"Now, Aunt Edna. We didn't come
over here to start any trouble." I
heard Harley Ann say.

Well, crap! Was the entire town
of Mercy hanging around my hospital
room? Not being able to see was far
more stressful than I'd ever realized.

I cleared my throat. "Could
someone tell me who all is here?"

"Just the three of us." Dixie
replied.

"Well thank goodness! I was

starting to wonder if everyone in town was standing here gawking at me." I heard the nasty note in my voice and felt bad. It wasn't their fault I was in this predicament.

"The sheriff called me and Aunt Edna, Lily Gayle." Harley Ann said in a soft voice, as though she understood my predicament and wanted to sooth my nerves. "He wasn't sure how long you're gonna be in here and thought we might figure out some shifts so that at least one of us is here with you at all times."

"Tell us exactly what happened, Lily Gayle." Miss Edna insisted. "There's got to be an explanation for this."

"The doctor said it's hysterical blindness." Dixie said.

"I'm right here. And I'm blind, not deaf." I said.

"Uh. Does hysterical, in this

situation, mean funny ha-ha or crazy." Harley Ann asked.

"It's doctor-talk for we don't have any idea but don't want to tell you that." Said Miss Edna.

I laughed. "That sounds like it's probably true."

"Of course it is. No doctor worth his salt is going to admit he's stumped."

I heard chair legs dragging across the floor and Dixie said, "Sit down, Miss Edna. There no call for you to stand."

"I'll take the chair. Because age has its privileges."

I held in a laugh, glad that she'd come after all. She had a great bedside manner.

"While we're all sittin' here, why don't we discuss the case?" Miss Edna said.

"Why not?" I said. "It'll pass the

time and maybe with four heads in the game we'll spot something."

I filled in the three of them on everything I'd learned about Angela, Samantha Taylor, Sandra Goodwyn and her mother and the vampire doll.

"Fool woman." Miss Edna muttered about Angela. "She could set off everybody in town running around in a fortune-teller wagon and gypsy clothes. I hope she stays gone."

"Are you saying you think one of these people is responsible for Larry gettin' killed?" she added.

"They seem to be the best candidates at this point. They all had access to the information about the secret study even though they deny it." I scratched my chin, thinking. "But I can't quite figure out the why. Or the bite marks on Larry's neck."

"I agree." Dixie threw in. "I don't see the connection to Larry.

Unless it's because he lived alone and would be easier to manipulate. I imagine he was grateful for any company he could get."

"Yes. But to what end?" Harley Ann asked. "What did one of them gain from it?"

None of us had an answer.

"I feel right bad that I never noticed any marks on Larry's neck when I took food to him." Miss Edna said, a sad note in her voice. "Maybe if I'd noticed them, he would still be here today."

"What makes you say that?" I asked.

"Because if I'd found out what was going on, I'd've gone straight to the sheriff with it."

"Don't beat yourself up, Miss Edna." Dixie said. "You weren't the only one taking him food were you? The others didn't notice either."

"Well that don't make me feel a bit better, Dixie Newsom." Miss Edna snapped.

A charged silence descended on the room after that statement. I sure didn't know what to say. I'd've felt just like Miss Edna if I'd missed something like that happening to a friend.

"Well. I'm ready to go home for the evening." Miss Edna broke the silence stretching between us. "I need to check on my flowers I'm planning on entering in the flower show. All this talk about Mary Goodwyn reminded me she's some pretty tough competition. But if any of you tell her I said that, I'll deny it to my grave."

"She had some beautiful poinsettias in the vet office when I went by there today." I said. "It seemed wrong somehow to see them in September."

"Did you touch them?" Miss Edna asked in an excited voice. "The leaves in particular."

"No. I just admired them from the chair where I was sitting." I leaned forward in the bed, toward Miss Edna's voice. "Why?"

"If you touch poinsettia leaves and then rub your eyes it can make you temporarily blind."

I fell back against the pillows, deflated. "That can't be the answer. I never touched them."

"Come on, Harley Ann. Let's get to the house. We'll be back in the morning so you can go home and rest, Dixie."

I heard footsteps leaving the room.

"You still here?" I inquired. Meaning Dixie.

Her hand touched my forearm where it rested on the bed beside my body.

"Yes. You try and get some rest. Close your eyes and maybe that'll help with the problem. Or maybe that wash they used on them will kick in and clear them up."

I woke up some time later, unsure how long I'd been asleep. It took me a couple of minutes to realize I could see pale gray in the blackness I'd been seeing before. I could see the vague outline of someone slumped in the bedside chair. Dixie. A tiny snore broke the silence and I grinned.

I wasn't going to be blind permanently. I wanted to wake Dixie up and celebrate, but I knew she'd been tuckered out earlier. And had no idea how long she might have been asleep.

I lay back thinking over the puzzle pieces of the murder, trying to fit some of them together into a picture that made sense.

Someone who had it in for the townsfolk who tested positive for the vampire gene had to be behind it all. So, going from that, and knowing it took a bit for the test results to come back, it must be someone who'd been involved with the study in the early days.

Who, besides Larry Gordon, had tested positive for the genetic anomaly? I strained my memory to recall who I'd heard mentioned as being early participants in the sleep apnea study. They'd be the first ones tested for the anomaly too.

Sadly, even though this was the biggest thing to happen in Mercy in decades, I just hadn't paid close attention to the gossip in the beginning about people taking part. I mean, really, sleep apnea. How boring.

Of my suspect list, I knew that Mary Goodwyn hadn't tested yet because she'd told me so. Now that I thought about it, I didn't know if Sandra Goodwyn had tested. However, I did know that Samantha Taylor *had* tested, but not what her results were. She was playing them close to the vest according to Doc Johnson. Could it be because she'd tested positive and didn't want anyone to know? Or maybe because she just didn't want people knowing her personal business. The Taylors tended to fall into the second category as a group. And I shuddered to think how her brothers might react if she'd tested positive and they found out. They weren't the most open-minded folks around.

I sighed and shifted in the bed. This was getting me nowhere. This was getting me nowhere fast and my eyelids felt heavy.

CHAPTER EIGHTEEN

When I opened my eyes again, I saw Dixie standing next to my bed. Kind of blurry, but I could recognize her.

I smiled at her.

"You can see me?" She asked, excitement dancing through her voice.

"Yes. You're blurry, but I can see you well enough to know who you are."

"This is fantastic! I'm going to call the doctor."

I grabbed her wrist. "Don't. Not yet."

"Why not?" She asked with a puzzled look.

"As long as I'm in here, our suspects think I'm out of commission. I don't want them to know I'm about to get back on the trail."

She sat in the chair next to my bed, doubt written all over her face. "Well. Okay. If that's how you want to handle it."

Samantha Taylor stuck her head in the door and I pretended not to see her.

"Hi Dixie. Hi, Lily Gayle. It's Samantha Taylor in case you don't recognize my voice. I'm just stopping by to see how you're doing this morning."

I made a big deal out of rolling my head side-to-side on the pillow and sighing. "About the same, Samantha. Thank you kindly for stopping by." I said.

"Is there anything I can get either of you?" She offered. "Some coffee or a breakfast biscuit?"

"I'm not hungry." I said. "Are you, Dixie? You can go on with Samantha if you want to get a bite. I'll be fine here for a little while."

"No. No. I'm fine, too." Dixie said.

"Okay." Samantha said. "None so blind as those who can't see."

"What?" I asked. Struggling to sit up in the bed. "What did you just say?"

I saw her shift her eyes around like she regretted saying it. But, I continued to act like I couldn't see.

"Oh. Sorry about that. I didn't mean anything by it." She gave an embarrassed little laugh. "It's just something that Sandra says all the time. I guess I picked it up from her."

I waved my hand around in her general direction. "No harm done. I was just curious."

"Okay, then. I'm headed to see if Doctor Johnson needs me this morning."

She disappeared around the corner of the door.

"Check the hallway." I hissed at Dixie. "Make sure she's gone."

Dixie stood up and peeked around the door facing. "She's almost to the end of the hall. Aaaand, now she's gone."

Dixie turned to face me. "What in tarnation are you up to?"

I threw the bedsheets aside. "Hand me my clothes. We've got to get out of here."

She pulled my clothes from the closet where she must've hung them last night. Thank goodness she was here. I shucked out of the hospital gown and got into my clothes as quickly as I could.

"Okay. We're not waiting for a doctor to come sign me out. We don't have time. I've got to call Vlad and tell him he's in danger. Then we have to get up to the Midnight Dragonfly. Sandra Goodwyn is the killer and she's working up there part time. She may try to take Vlad out if we don't get him out of there and she realizes the jig is up."

I peered around the door. The hallway was empty. Good. I motioned Dixie to follow me. "We can call Ben on the way and give him a heads up. He can meet us there."

"Wait." Dixie huffed along next to me. "How do you know it's Sandra Goodwyn all of a sudden?"

"She said that phrase to me yesterday when I was at the animal clinic. Right after she was being a horse's ass about my genealogical research. Saying she was surprised that I hadn't uncovered the fact that the Taylors are kin to the Mitchells on the wrong side of the blanket."

"What? *Really*? How did she know that?"

"Not important right this minute. I'll explain that part later. But, she also works at the sleep study inputting data for Vlad. She's only supposed to be working with the sleep study data, but I bet she figured out how to access other stuff on the computer and stumbled onto the vampire gene testing."

I stopped at the door leading out into the waiting room. No way we could exit the building without going through there. Right past the nurses station. Well, crap.

"Let's walk slow through here and out the door. Maybe the nurses won't realize it's me until it's too late to try and stop me. We don't have time to deal with them right now."

We strolled through the waiting room like we belonged. Luck was a lady and we made it safely out the doors and into the parking lot.

"Where's your car?"

Dixie pointed to the left. I squinted and spotted the Taurus tucked into a spot at the other end of the lot. Great.

"Let's go. I rummaged in my purse as we walked, found my cellphone and punched Vlad's number.

It went to voicemail and I could've screamed in frustration.

Vlad. It's Lily Gayle. Get out of the house and find a safe place out of sight. Sandra Goodwyn is the killer. She may come after you. Call me when you get this message.

We hopped into Dixie's car. She threw me back against the seat as she took off burning rubber out of the parking lot.

"What?" she asked when I shot her a look. "You said we're in a hurry."

I punched Ben's number on my phone. Voicemail. Where the heck was everybody?

CHAPTER NINETEEN

As we drove through town at a much higher speed than the thirty-five that was the posted limit, I noticed the town was eerily deserted.

"Hey, Dix. I don't see anyone out and about. What do you think that's about?"

Dixie slowed down a bit as we came to the town square and rolled to a halt. Todd had his patrol car parked across the road leading out of town. He stepped out of it and held up his hand in the classic halt move as Dixie eased forward a bit.

I felt a nervous giggle rise up in my throat and swallowed it back down. It felt as though we'd somehow stumbled into an alternate universe. Dixie glanced at me, then past me.

"I don't see any cars at all." She squinted. "And it looks like my shop is closed. Sarah's gonna be in a world of trouble once we get this situation straightened out. She promised me she'd take care of everything at the shop today til I could get over there for my first appointment at two this afternoon."

Todd walked up to the car and Dixie rolled down her window. Todd leaned over and glanced at me.

"Thought you were still in the hospital, Lily Gayle." He said.

"I just got out." I told him. "Dixie's taking me home."

He shifted his gaze to Dixie. "You were going mighty fast for someone taking a friend home from the hospital."

"For Heaven's sake, Todd. What's with the interrogation? And why do you have the road blocked? I want to get home and this is the only road to get there."

Todd adjusted his hat and squinted at me. "There's a situation the sheriff is taking care of and told me to keep the road blocked off. You'll have to go to Dixie's for now."

My blood pressure shot up about a hundred points at that news. I made eye contact with Dixie.

She shook her head and mouthed *No*.

I frowned and jerked my head in the direction of the road.

She shook her head again.

"Be reasonable, Dixie." Todd said. "There's no call for the two of you to get involved in the sheriff's business. Y'all will just be a distraction for him."

Dixie's head turned very slowly toward Todd. "What did you just say to me?"

Uh oh. Todd had messed up now. He seemed to realize that as he back-pedaled.

"Now, Dixie. You know I didn't mean anything personal about that. I'd say the same thing to anyone trying to get past this here blockade."

"Are you going to move your car so I can take my sick friend to her home?" Dixie asked in her sweetest voice.

"Now, Dixie -"

Dixie floored the gas, jerking the steering wheel to the right. I clutched the door handle like my life depended on it. Which it might depending on Dixie's ability to squeeze past the squad car sitting in front of us.

Both hands white-knuckling the wheel, Dixie jumped the curb and swung around the patrol car without so much as a scratch. We bounced back down onto the street and headed out of town. Dixie stuck one arm and the window. I didn't know if she was waving or flipping him the bird.

His shocked face was all I could see in the side view mirror.

I laughed out loud.

"I sure never thought you'd do that, Dixie."

She glanced over at me. "You know I hate when people try to tell me what to do. And then when they imply I'm going to cause more trouble than I'm worth, I really get mad."

I leaned forward watching the road like I could see through trees and figure out what was going on at the

Midnight Dragonfly. That had to be where Ben was taking care of a 'situation' as Todd described it.

As though reading my mind, Dixie said. "Do you think something bad is going on up at the sleep study?"

"Yes. I got voice mail when I tried to call both Ben and Vlad. They may be busy with other things and just couldn't answer their phones. But with that roadblock back there, I'm wondering how bad it is."

CHAPTER TWENTY

As the car careened onto the long driveway leading up to the Midnight Dragonfly, Dixie stood on the brakes.

Mary Goodwyn stood in the middle of the driveway. Obviously in a bad way. Her hair snarled around her face and she looked like she'd just grabbed clothes and threw them on. Nothing matched. Even her shoes. One a running shoe and the other a dress flat.

She turned at the sound of Dixie's squealing brakes. We managed to stop two feet from hitting her. She never made the first move to get out of the way. Our eyes met through windshield and hers went wide.

She rushed to the passenger side of the car and motioned for me to roll down the window.

"Can you see me?" She asked in a breathless voice.

I nodded cautiously, not wanting to startle her.

She wailed out loud, scaring me half to death.

Dixie leaned over to look out the window and said, "Get in the car, Mary. We're headed up to the house to see what's going on. We think Vlad and Ben might be in trouble. I don't want to leave you here by yourself looking like this."

Mary continued to stare at me. Then said. "You were supposed to be out of commission for a while longer."

"What?" I said.

"I put some ground up poinsettia leaves and stem on top of your cookies hoping you'd touch them. And you did. You rubbed them between your fingers and I just knew my plan was going to work."

Dixie and I exchanged looks.

"What plan was that, Mary?"

"You're so darn nosy. And smart. And I knew you were at the clinic trying to find some clues and that business about writing about the founding families was nothing but your cover."

"What did you do, Mary?" Dixie asked quietly.

"I figured. I hoped. I prayed. That Lily Gayle would touch those ground up leaves and then rub her eyes at some point before she washed her hands. Poinsettias have a substance on them that, if you rub your eyes after you've touched them, will make you temporarily blind. I just wanted to put you out of commission for a few days."

She began crying quietly.

"Get in the car, Mary. We'll take care of you. There's nothing to worry about. Lily Gayle is okay."

Mary shook her head and darted off into the woods next to the driveway.

"I have to stop Sandra!" She shouted over her shoulder. "I can't let you two stop me."

I watched her fade into the tree line.

"She must have known, or suspected, that Sandra was behind everything." Dixie said.

I turned my eyes away from the woods. "Not soon enough to save Larry Gordon, though. Let's get on up there and see what's what. I don't want Ben or Vlad to get hurt if we can help stop it."

As we rounded the final curve in

the long driveway, Dixie slammed on the brakes again.

A mob, on foot, blocked the driveway and spilled onto the lawn of the mansion.

Raised voices shouted for Vlad to come out, but I didn't see him anywhere in sight.

"Have *mercy!*" Dixie breathed.

I opened the car door and Dixie grabbed my wrist before I could get out. "You are not getting out of this car."

I glanced at the mob surging in front of us and knew she was right. There was no way I'd be able to get through them.

"What do you suggest? We can't let them get to Vlad."

"Shut the door."

When I did, she threw the car in reverse. We got some looks as we backed out of the driveway, but no one made any move in our direction.

"Where are we going?"

"I'm going to get us as close as possible to our old hang out. Then we're going to hike up through the woods to the house. I'm not sure yet how we're going to get across the yard, but unless you've got a better idea, I'm going with this one."

"Lead on, MacDuff." I said.

I tried to call both men again and got voicemail again. We were on our own. Mostly likely Ben was lurking somewhere near the crowd trying to figure out how he was going to disperse that mob.

By the time we'd climbed to the last of the trees behind the house I was out of breath and sweating. We crouch behind some bushes to assess the situation.

Death said the Gypsy Queen

This close we could make out some of the shouting. And they were talking about torching the house.

CHAPTER TWENTY TWO

Dixie and I exchanged looks.

"We've got to get up there and put a stop to this."

"What do you think the two of us can do?" Dixie inquired.

"I don't know, but we've got to try."

I gauged the distance from the tree line to the back porch. Most of the crowd had gathered directly in front of the house. If we made our way directly behind, we'd have a chance.

As we worked our way along the the tree line toward the back of the house, bushes rustled to our right. I held in a scream and clapped a hand over Dixie's mouth when I heard her draw a deep breath. She bit my hand and I let go.

Ben and Todd stepped out of the bushes.

"I should've known you two would be showing up." He gave me a hard look. "I thought you were blind and safely tucked away in the hospital."

"As you can see. I'm recovered and Dixie and I are here to help."

"I tried to stop them at the road block, Sheriff. But, they went right around my car." Todd said.

Ben shook his head.

"I don't know what you think the two of you can accomplish against that crowd. I called for reinforcements from Clay county and Todd and I are laying low till they get here."

He motioned to the bushes behind him. "You two are going to wait with us. There's nothing we can do right now."

"Look." Todd said, pointing to the house.

I gulped when I saw what he'd pointed out. Sandra Goodwyn had Vlad by the collar of his shirt and was holding him upright in front of the mob.

"Here's the traitor!" I heard her shout. "Here's the man looking for the abominations among us and keeping their secret."

A roar went up from the crowd and it surged closer to the steps leading up to where Sandra and Vlad stood.

"Torch it!" I heard someone shout and Ben groaned next to me. In agony because there was nothing he could do but wait for a possible opportunity to save his friend.

A dozen people scattered toward the woods. Ben and Todd pulled Dixie and me into deeper cover as we watched helplessly.

The individuals ran back toward the house with dead tree limbs in hand. A lighter passed hand to hand as we watched in horror. Flames licked up the dead wood held high and flames hissed as the torches arched toward the house.

I struggled to break Ben's grip on my arm. "Let go. We have to get up there and save Vlad and the people inside!"

"There's no one inside. Vlad told me yesterday he was going to send everyone home this morning. And stop testing until the murder was solved. Thank goodness he did."

The torches began to burn out as we watched. The steps and porch of the old mansion were marble. The wood burned itself out. I thought maybe we'd make it until back up arrived.

But then, one man lit another torch and with a loud scream ran straight up to the house and tossed the torch through an open ground floor window. Others followed suit.

Flames licked up the draperies, lighting up the waning afternoon with red.

"Dammit!" Ben agonized. "Where is that back up?"

Sandra got Vlad in a neck lock and knocked his feet out from under him. Why wasn't he fighting back? Sandra wasn't a big girl. He should be able to break free easily.

Then I noticed his head lolling to the side. Eyes barely open. She must have dosed him with something.

"Ben." I said. "We've got to get up there and get Vlad away from her."

"No. We'll all end up as targets if we rush up there now. Just wait. We have to choose the perfect moment."

I turned back to watch the scene. Sandra shouted to the crowd. "Yes! Burn the house. Burn the place where abominations hid among us!"

From the corner of my eye, I saw a woman running across the lawn. Mary Goodwyn.

She rushed up the steps, grabbed her daughter by the shoulders and rapped her head against a marble column. Vlad slumped to the ground.

As Ben, Todd, Dixie and I ran toward the house, blue lights burst into the clearing along the sides of the driveway and six police cars came to a halt, spilling officers holding riot gear and weapons. The crowd disperses like magic. All running in different directions with officers in hot pursuit.

Ben and I raced up the steps to the porch, grabbed Vlad and supported him back down to the lawn. Mary Goodwyn appeared from the opposite direction and dragged her daughter down the steps behind us. Flames licked against the front door and bloomed from all of the first floor windows.

Sirens blared as two fire trucks ground up the driveway. Hoses were unrolled and dragged to the pond behind the house and hooked to the pumper truck. But we all knew it was too late to save the house. All the firemen could accomplish at this point was to keep it contained to the house.

Dixie and I waited and watched their effort with Vlad at our feet while Ben and Todd went to bring the cars up. There was no way Vlad could walk out of here.

Death said the Gypsy Queen

As we loaded him in Dixie's car,
I glanced back over my shoulder in time
to see a corner of the roof crash in.

CHAPTER TWENTY THREE

"The old Mitchell Manor, recently being called by the ridiculous name of Midnight Dragonfly, is gone, I suppose." Commented Miss Edna as Dixie and I sat with her and Harley Ann on her big front porch a week later.

"Yes." Dixie said. "So sad. That house stood there for a long time. And saw a lot of changes."

"And shielded a lot of secrets." I added.

Death said the Gypsy Queen

Miss Enda sniffed. "So tell me again why Sandra Goodwyn went crazy?"

I shook my head. Sometimes the woman just had no couth at all.

I settled back in my rocking chair, setting it in motion. "Her mama told us she'd been fascinated by vampire and werewolf books and movies for years and then all of a sudden turned against them. No rhyme or reason. She was taking Sandra to see a psychiatrist up in Memphis, but even that wasn't helping much."

"And what was going on with Larry Gordon?" Harley Ann asked. "What was the deal with the puncture marks on his neck?"

I sighed. "That was Sandra playing games. She'd become both fascinated and repulsed by the whole vampire thing. When she discovered the secret files Vlad had on the DNA testing, she thought it was her chance to finally understand her obsession. She managed to break the code to access the information and found out that Larry had tested positive for the vampire gene."

I took a drink of tea to wet my throat and went on.

"She started going out to his house and hanging around with him trying to understand what the vampire gene meant. And then she decided to start biting him and drinking his blood to see if she could turn herself into a vampire."

I glanced around at my audience. Everything seemed so normal sitting here on the porch today. But, I didn't doubt for a minute that there was still a bunch of muttering and unrest running underground throughout the town about the murder. And about Vlad and his no-longer-secret testing.

It just went to show that we don't truly know what goes on behind closed doors.

"She lured poor Larry out there to the farmer's market site by telling him she needed help getting her mama's booth set up early so she could go work at the clinic while her mama handled the booth. At least that's what she told Ben. He said she didn't seem to understand that there was anything wrong with what she did."

I shuddered to think what poor old Larry's last moments must have been like.

"I imagine he had no reason to think it was odd for her to ask for his help. It probably never occurred to him that he was in danger from his friend."

Dixie shook her head. "I can't believe no one noticed how sick she was."

"She hid it well." I said. "She and her mama have moved to an undisclosed town to a clinic there that can treat her until she's deemed competent to stand trial. The judge ordered it after a psychiatrist said she wasn't competent."

"Did you find out who put that weird doll on your porch?" Harley Ann shuddered. "That was so creepy!"

I picked up a biscuit out of the linen covered basket on the table and slathered vanilla honey butter on it as I answered. "It was Mary. She was trying to warn me about her daughter."

Miss Edna made a rude sound. "Sounds like some of that passive aggressive mess I hear about on TV. If she thought her daughter was involved, why didn't she go straight to Ben with it? Or take her somewhere she could get some help since that psychiatrist in Memphis wasn't having any effect on her. Or even come to one of us. Lord knows everyone in town knows we'd help anyone in trouble."

"Sometimes people do the wrong things for the right reasons." Said Dixie, always the peacemaker.

"Tell that to Larry Gordon." Snapped Miss Edna.

There was no good answer to that, so to change the subject, I pointed to a quilt lying over a wicker loveseat on the porch. "That's an unusual quilt pattern. I don't think I've ever seen it before."

"Isn't it beautiful?" Harley Ann went over and picked up the quilt. "I found it in Aunt Edna's attic the other day."

She handed it to me and sat back down.

I examined the quilt. From the actual cotton poking out through some small tears in the fabric, I knew it was very old. The hand stitching was also a clue. I stood and held it as open as I could. It was incredibly heavy because of the actual cotton filling.

"Harley Ann, could you help me hold this up? I want to see the overall pattern."

Harley Ann complied and we gazed at the pattern revealed. It still didn't look familiar to me. Plenty of colors and pieces that looked like they'd been taken from old clothing. Nothing unusual about that. But, interspersed through the color blocks were sections with two black triangles joined at one corner grouped together scattered across the quilt.

"Do those look like vampire teeth to y'all?" I asked.

"Good grief, Lily Gayle." Miss Edna said. "You've got vampires on the brain. It's just an old quilt."

Death said the Gypsy Queen

I glanced at Dixie who shrugged and shook her head.

"Speaking of vampires. How's Vlad doing?" Miss Edna wanted to know.

"He's not a vampire, Miss Edna. As you well know."

She cocked her head to the side. "Depends on who you ask."

"He's *not* a vampire." I insisted. "And he's going to be fine. Sandra injected him with a whooping dose of anesthetic to keep him under control so it's going to take a bit but he's going to fully recover."

I carefully folded the old quilt and placed it back on the loveseat.

"So. Are the two of you an item, now?" Miss Edna inquired with a smile.

"Maybe." I replied. "We'll see what the future brings on that one."

Cozy Chocolate Cobbler

Ingredients:

1 stick butter

1 cup sugar

1 cup self rising flour

1 tsp vanilla

1 cup milk

Chocolate layer ingredients:

1 cup sugar

5 Tablespoons cocoa powder

2 cups boiling water

Preheat oven to 350 degrees

Melt butter in 9 x 13 baking dish

In mixing bowl combine sugar, flour, vanilla and milk

Pour over melted butter. DO NOT STIR

In separate bowl combine cocoa and sugar from chocolate layer ingredients

Sprinkle over batter in baking dish. DO NOT STIR

Pour 2 cups boiling water over that. DO NOT STIR

Bake for 30 – 45 minutes. Until golden brown.

Death said the Gypsy Queen

Have Mercy Grilled Pimento Cheese Sandwich

Ingredients:

1 ½ cup shredded cheddar cheese

½ cup shredded swiss cheese

1 jar (7 oz) pimentos

1 cup mayonnaise

¼ teaspoon garlic powder

¼ teaspoon onion powder

2 teaspoons Worcestershire sauce

1 Large tomato

Loaf of French bread

Butter

Stir all ingredients together in a large bowl.

Slice French bread into about ½ inch thick slices

Slice tomato into thin slices

Spread pimento cheese on bread

Add tomato slice

Top with another piece of French bread

Butter outside of both pieces of bread

Place in hot skillet and cook until golden brown on both sides

Excerpt from Death of a Wolfman (Book 1 in the Lily Gayle Lambert Mysteries)

CHAPTER ONE

Last time I checked I wasn't in the family way. So why was the local midwife coming up my front walk? It sure looked like LizBeth Mitchell. You couldn't miss that white-blond hair of hers shining like a beacon in the morning sun. The kind of hair my mama used to call towhead.

I couldn't think of a single reason she would be here. Unless she was delivering somebody's baby she didn't go to other people's houses. They might be dirty or have germs or something. When she was delivering a baby she looked like she had wandered out of a big-city operating room, she had so much protective gear on.

And, darn it, I had been just about to get dressed for my weekly dinner date with the county sheriff, who also happened to be my cousin. I sighed. It'd have to wait till I found out the reason for this visit. I just hoped it wouldn't take long. Ben hated it when I was late.

The antique doorbell made its hideous grinding noise just as I pulled myself out of my favorite overstuffed club chair. My teeth clamped together in protest. That bell sounded worse than fingernails on a chalkboard and friends knew better than to use the old thing.

I'd taken half a dozen steps when the doorbell growled again, startling me so much I almost dropped my glass of sweet tea. *Crap, LizBeth. Give a body time to get to the door, why don't you?*

Peeking out the slightly frosted glass panel next to the door, I observed my visitor in secret. LizBeth had a frown on her face as she scanned the front porch. OK, so it needed to be sanded and a fresh coat of paint applied. In a fit of mild embarrassment, I decided I'd have to sweet-talk Ben into taking care of that. My fear of heights crippled me so bad I couldn't even wear stiletto heels; getting on a stepladder to paint the ceiling of the big front porch didn't even fall into the realm of possibility.

Running a quick hand through my hair, I looked down at my bare feet, cropped pants and stretched out T-shirt. Not the kind of outfit to wear for receiving company, but those who dropped by without calling first would have to take me the way I was.

Putting on my company smile, I eased the door open. It squealed just a tiny bit and LizBeth jumped. *Nervous little thing, wasn't she?* I made a mental note to put some WD-40 on the hinges. WD-40 and duct tape, the single—or, in my case, widowed—woman's best friends.

"Hey there, LizBeth. Come on in." As she stepped in, I asked, "Can I get you a glass of sweet tea? I made some fresh just a little while ago."

"That won't be necessary, but thank you."

"Uh. OK, then. Why don't we take a seat in the front room here?"

LizBeth sat on the edge of a small

couch by the dead fireplace, hands clasped in her lap, so I took the wingback chair next to it instead of my beloved cushy chair by the window.

Silence dragged on. I squashed the urge to fidget. *What on earth was LizBeth doing here?* I watched the other woman's eyes roam the room and tried to see it as a stranger would myself.

The marble surround on the fireplace had a few nicks and scratches, as did the mantel my great-grandfather had carved out of oak more than a hundred years ago. But it gleamed with the beeswax polish of four generations of loving hands. The floors really needed to be refinished, but I kept putting that off. Besides, the antique Aubusson rugs hid the worst spots, even though the rugs were worn a little thin from foot traffic.

And in the corner stood my antique dressmaker's dummy, sporting the half-finished Renaissance gown I was making for a customer. Snips of fabric and a scatter of threads surrounded the project. I hadn't cleaned up last night after working on the dress.

Mentally, I gave myself a shake. Why was I letting this woman make me uncomfortable in my own home?

"Er. Is there something I can do for you?"

LizBeth jerked her eyes back. "Oh. I'm sorry. I guess my mind wandered for a minute there. You have a lovely home. So cozy."

"Thank you." *Even though your eyes are saying something different.*

"Really. It seems like a real home. Where real people live. Not a big, cold showplace like our house." LizBeth showed her teeth in what she must have thought was a friendly smile, but it didn't quite make it there.

I thought about the Gothic-style granite monstrosity sitting on a hill above town. It did look kind of cold from the outside. But some truly breathtaking architecture all the same. Legend had it slaves had hauled the granite from an old quarry five miles away to build the house, and the owner at the time had hired the best architect in Philadelphia to design the house. At a time when this part of

Mississippi had been considered the Wild West.

LizBeth broke into my thoughts. "I guess you're wondering why I'm here."

"No. Not at all. It's nice of you to come by and visit." *Even though if somebody had told me you'd ever step foot through the door I'd've called them a liar.*

"Come on, Lily Gayle...I can call you Lily Gayle?"

I nodded.

"We both know this isn't a social visit. I've come to ask you to do a genealogical research project on my family."

I gulped.

"I'm willing to pay your going rate. Whatever it costs."

Something didn't feel right about this. The Mitchells were the most reclusive family around.

Susan Boles

is the USA Today and Wall Street Journal Bestselling author of the Lily Gayle Lambert Mystery Series and a contributing author to the Brotherhood Protectors World.

A lifelong long love of all things mysterious led Susan to write cozy mysteries. Nancy Drew and Trixie Belden were the first to show her that girls can be crime solvers. Agatha Christie showed her that even small towns have big secrets. And Phryne Fisher showed her lady detectives can be outrageously individual. She lives in Mississippi with her rescue mini dachshund, Lucy, and her rescue cat of no particular breed, Zimba. She currently writes the Lily Gayle Lambert mystery series set in the fictional town of Mercy, Mississippi featuring a multi-generational cast of female sleuths and romantic suspense in the Brotherhood Protectors Kindle World.

Visit her website at www.susanbolesauthor.com

Death said the Gypsy Queen

www.ingramcontent.com/pod-product-compliance
Lightning Source LLC
Chambersburg PA
CBHW031232120726
47905CB00002B/562